Pact with the Pack

Bargains Struck Book 1

AJ Mullican

Dedication

This book is dedicated to the classic *Red Riding Hood* tale by Charles Perrault, which loosely inspired my story. It's dedicated to the reverse harem author and reader communities, who have shown me that you don't always have to choose, to my husband, who tolerated me spending hours upon hours churning this out, to the stupid pandemic for giving me that extra time to dedicate, and to all my fans out there. You guys encourage me to keep going!

Chapter 1

If I can't have you, Cherry, no one can.

Pretty standard ex-boyfriend threat, and if not for the switchblade that narrowly missed my jugular a week ago, I might not be worried. Eric did have the switchblade, however, and, though the cops confiscated it when they arrested him, now that he's out on bail it would be no problem for him to find another one.

The venom and possessiveness in his voice replay in my head as I see the words repeated on my phone screen. I changed my number the day after Eric tried to kill me, but despite reassurances from everyone I know that they wouldn't give him the new one, he got hold of it from somewhere. Now, not even an hour after the district attorney called to warn me that Eric slipped his ankle monitor and disappeared, he's texting me threats.

I've gotta get out of town.

Fear grips me tight as I shove my arms in my red leather bike jacket and jam the cherry-red helmet on my head. I rev up my motorcycle, and the tires squeal as I peel out of the parking lot outside my apartment.

I can't stay here anymore; Eric will be coming for me.

With no family except my grandma, Ethel, I speed through the heavy downtown North Carolina traffic on my way to her cabin in the woods, just outside of Nowhere. My auburn braid bounces in the wind, threatening to work its way free of the hair tie holding my curls in place.

Traffic thins the farther I get from town, and by the time I arc the bike onto Old Country Road at the edge of the woods, the streets lie empty behind me. I allow my shoulders to relax, and I give in to the purr of the engine and the gentle bumping of the less-maintained concrete as the bike speeds through the path between the dense trees. Hazy moonlight slips through the foliage, creating a strobe-like effect on my visor.

Granny Ethel lives on a dirt road that veers from the pavement at a sharp angle, and I skid on some loose rocks when I take the turn. The motorcycle wobbles, but I regain control and slow the bike down to avoid a wreck in the middle of nowhere.

If I didn't have a psycho ex-boyfriend out to kill me, I'd be better able to appreciate the beauty of the forest around me. Light streams down through the breaks in the trees to pool in patches on the ground that remind me of a Pollack panting, illuminating the greens and browns and greys of nature.

One particular set of greys lying on a fallen oak at the side of the road strikes me so much that I stop the bike and idle in awe.

Not twenty yards away lies the biggest, most beautiful wolf I've ever seen. The engine of the bike does nothing to scare it away; if anything, the cock of its head and perked-up ears indicate a level of curiosity.

I know better than to dismount and approach the majestic beast, but something draws me to it all the same, trapping me in its gaze. Its crystal-blue eyes bore into me through the helmet, as though it can see

straight through the tinted visor into my soul. Its snout
bobs, sniffing the air, and its tail thumps the tree in a
wag that, were it a neighborhood dog, might entice me
to go try to pet it.

Then I remember the scar on my neck, stitches
freshly out this morning and still bright red just a week
after Eric's attack, and I decide I quite like my neck in
one piece. I start the bike back down the road to
Granny Ethel's with a wave in the direction of the wolf.

Twenty minutes later I pull into the gravel drive
outside Granny's cottage, and my blood runs cold at
the sight of Eric's car parked there.

Worse yet, the door to the cabin sits ajar, and I
don't see Eric anywhere outside.

The bushes to either side of the drive rustle in the
night wind, but otherwise I detect no movement
outside the cabin. Granny Ethel's car sits in its usual
spot by the house, and in the bike's headlights I see
slashed tires on the old Caddy.

Shit.

The last thing I want to do is go into that cabin.
Eric's most likely inside, waiting to finish what he
started a week ago, but if Granny Ethel's car is here,
then she is, too. I can't leave her alone in there with
him. I cut the bike's engine, put down the kickstand,
and swing my leg over the back to dismount.

Unlike Eric, I don't own any knives. I don't have a
gun. I have nothing to defend myself with.

Neither does Granny, though, and that's what
matters now.

Despite the decreased visibility, I keep the helmet
on. Something about that extra layer combined with the
thickness of the leather motorcycle jacket provides a

small comfort, like I'm wearing armor.

I creep to the door, my heeled boots crunching in the gravel. Even with the helmet muffling everything, it echoes like gunshots in the night. In a distant, rational part of my mind, I wonder why I try to be stealthy. The motorcycle announced my arrival.

Eric already knows I'm here.

The stairs up to the porch creak with even my sleight weight, and each step makes me cringe. So loud. Why does Granny's porch have to be so loud?

Her front door hinges aren't much better. They squeal as I nudge the door further open. Light streams through the open door, but the front room lies vacant. Well, vacant save for a broken glass, some upturned furniture, and a smeared blood trail that leads into the back bedroom.

Granny...

My instincts scream at me to run, to get the fuck out of there before Eric comes out of the bedroom to kill me, but I don't know if Granny Ethel is still alive. If there's even the slightest chance, I can't leave her.

I sidestep the blood and pick up the biggest shard of glass from the floor. It might not be much, but it's better than the nothing I had before. At least my gloves keep me from slicing my own damn hand on the thing. I clench it tight to stop the trembling and creep down the short hallway, cursing the heavy moto boots I have on. *Clomp. Clomp. Clomp.* Terrible for sneaking on hardwood floors.

The blood trail goes under the door, which Eric left cracked, and through the slit between the door and the jamb I see more blood pooled next to the bed. I still can't see Granny Ethel, though.

I take a deep breath, stand off to the side of the doorway, and kick the door open with the toe of my boot.

A nightmare greets me on the other side. Eric stands over Granny Ethel's body, which has a jagged gash in her throat so deep it makes me gag at the sight. The knife in Eric's hand drips my grandma's blood, and its serrated blade measures almost the length of my forearm.

Suddenly, the shard of glass in my hand doesn't seem any better than nothing.

I scream and try to back up, to run, but Eric moves too fast. Before I know it, he's got my arm in a vicelike grip, causing me to drop the glass shard, and for the second time in a week he holds a blade to my throat.

"Hey, Cherry." Even through the helmet, Eric reeks of liquor, which doesn't surprise me; he was drunk for most of our relationship. He leans into me until his body presses me against the wall. "I missed you, baby. Why don't you take that stupid helmet off so I can look into your beautiful green eyes?"

Take off my armor? No way. I'd shake my head, but fear paralyzes me.

He holds the knife tighter against my neck. The leather jacket's protecting me so far, but the teeth on the blade can saw through it in no time, I'm sure, and I have no avenue of escape right now.

"Take. It. Off." Eric's voice comes out in a growl, and I know it's not a matter of *if* he kills me tonight, but how long he'll take to do it.

Shit.

I move slow so as not to further provoke him, and his hand moves from my arm to my shoulder so I can get the helmet off. Wisps of curly hair tickle my face as they fall free of the helmet. I meet Eric's bloodshot eyes, and the malice in them as he smiles at me sends a chill down my spine.

"There you are." He moves to cup my cheek with his free hand, but the touch has no affection to it. "You know you're mine, right, Cherry? I was your first, Cherry. No one else can have what I have with you. That creates a bond, Cherry. You might think you can cheat with however many men you want, but you'll always be mine."

I should know better than to get snarky, but the way he keeps repeating my name pisses me off. "It wasn't cheating, Eric. We broke up."

The hand on my cheek slides down to grip my throat, and the blade moves to hover over my heart. "We. Have. A. *Bond*." He pokes my jacket with the tip of the knife. "Right here. You can't break up with the kind of bond we have, Cherry."

My heart pounds underneath the tip of Eric's blade, and he holds my neck so tight I feel my pulse in my throat. It's getting harder to breathe, and stars twinkle in the edges of my vision.

"I'm going to remind you of our bond tonight, Cherry. I'm going to make sure you never forget who you belong to. Who you belong with. I was your first, Cherry, and I'll be your last. I am your forever."

I want to be brave. I want to fight back, but it takes all I have not to piss myself. He's got me pinned and choked, and I can't move except to tremble from head to toe. Hot tears stream down my cheeks.

"Please, Eric." I struggle to get the words out past the hand tightening on my throat. "Please don't do this.

Let's just call the cops right now. You can turn yourself in, and maybe if you let me go, they'll go easy on you in court. Two murder charges are worse than one. Maybe, if you don't hurt me again—"

He squeezes, and I gag. "Shut the *fuck* up, Cherry. You lost the right to plead for mercy when you slept around on me. You fucked other men, Cherry. I can't just forgive that."

He's insane. Eric's lost his fucking mind, and I'm going to die because he can't separate fantasy from reality.

Eric's lips spread in a wide grin as he slides the tip of the knife down the front of my jacket to my stomach. "This is going to hurt me more than it hurts you, Cherry, but it's necessary. I can't let you go on being tainted by other men. I'll fix you tonight, Cherry. I'll purify you, so you're all mine again, and once we're reunited you'll see. You'll see that I'm the one you're supposed to be with." The blade slides under the leather and under my tank top to press against the soft flesh of my belly. The sting on my skin brings back memories of a week ago, when his switchblade opened a thick line on my throat.

I can't help it; I cry out despite his chokehold.

My eyes widen at the feral growls that follow.

They don't come from Eric.

Chapter 2

Eric's gaze swivels towards the sound first, and when his pupils dilate and his grip on my neck loosens a fraction, I allow myself a glance as well.

The wolf from the side of the road stands in my grandma's hallway, teeth bared and hackles raised.

He's not alone.

Four more wolves crowd into the small cabin, all poised for attack.

If this wasn't a life-or-death situation, I might have taken the time to marvel at their grace and beauty despite their enormous size. I've seen wolves at the zoo, but these — these are *beasts*. Imagine an English Mastiff on steroids, only in the shape of a wolf. Any one of these wolves on their own easily outweighs Eric, and Eric's not a small man.

Eric whips the knife from under my shirt, cutting deep on his way out, and the cabin explodes in a blur of fur, fangs, and blood.

The first wolf lunges at Eric, which frees me to clutch my bleeding stomach and scurry into the bedroom. I want to slam the door shut, but the fight spills into the doorway behind me, and I realize I've just escaped one trap to encase myself in another. The bedroom window is too small for me to climb through, and the wolf's massive body fills my only exit. Even if I could get past it, the other wolves stand guard in the hallway, ready to catch Eric if he manages to run.

A sharp yelp pierces the air as Eric gets a lucky shot in on the wolf in front. He withdraws his knife, and a spray of dark blood splatters the bedroom wall. The wolf's not down for the count yet, though, and his jaws clamp down on Eric's neck.

Part of me finds a poetic justice in the carnage that ensues.

Part of me wants to puke as Eric's throat is ripped to shreds right in front of me.

Eric's body spasms for a few seconds before falling deathly still. A few spurts of blood still pump as his heart beats its last.

The bleeding wolf steps over Eric's corpse and stalks towards me. I've backed myself as far into the corner as I can, but I don't know why I'm even trying to get away. If Eric, at nearly twice my weight and armed with a knife, got mowed down by this beast in no time, I don't stand a chance.

I freeze as the wolf reaches me and extends his blood-soaked snout. Like he did in the woods earlier, he sniffs the air around me. He huffs and noses my stomach.

This is it. I'm going to die. He smells my blood, senses a weakness, and I'm about to be lunch. Eaten by wolves at my grandma's house in the woods—I'd laugh at the irony, if I thought I had time left to laugh.

Rather than eating me, though, the wolf whines and pushes my shirt and hands out of the way with his nose to lick my cut. He nuzzles my stomach and presses his uninjured shoulder against my hip. He throws his head back and howls, and the wolves in the hallway answer with howls of their own. A buzzing sensation surges through me, and I think maybe I've lost more blood than I realize.

I unzip my jacket and lift the hem of my soaked top to inspect the damage caused by Eric's blade. The six-inch-long cut oozes thick blood, so much so that I can't see how bad it is. I can't see anything in the opening that I can identify as an organ. It's still deep as fuck, though, deep enough that he could have nicked something vital, and I'm still going to die if I don't get to a hospital soon. I reach with a shaky hand to my back pocket and try to pull out my phone, but my glove is too slick with blood for me to grip the smooth surface of the device.

This last failure, this last little thing preventing me from getting help, breaks me. I sink into the corner and pull my knees to my chest as sobs wrack my body. My abdomen really fucking hurts when I cry, but I guess since I'll be dead soon it doesn't matter.

Something about near-death makes me brave, because I decide I want to spend my last moments on Earth snuggling the two-hundred-plus pound wolf beside me. I wrap my arms around his neck and sniffle into his soft fur, careful to avoid the gash in his shoulder.

I don't hear the police and paramedics arrive, but I open my eyes to four strange men standing in the room with me and the wolf.

I must be in shock; all four men look naked to my blurry, tear-filled eyes.

The closest and largest of the men crouches a couple feet away from the wolf's haunches and extends a hand. He's six-three, easy, and made of solid muscle. I don't see a single ounce of excess fat on his body at all. Sandy blonde hair falls into his dark blue eyes, making him look young, and if my blood-starved brain gauges right, I'd say he's in about his mid-twenties.

The other three men have a similar appearance, but each is still distinct enough to tell apart. The sexy tats they're sporting help me tell the difference, too. Six-Three squatting on the other side of the wolf, for instance, has what looks like a full traditional Maori sleeve on his left arm that extends onto his chest. Six-Two behind him has a flaming skull in the center of his chest and longer hair, Six-One has, ironically, a wolf on his shoulder, and Five-Ten in the back has some gorgeous watercolor floral work wrapped around his tight, muscular thigh.

Six-Three somehow manages to look at the wolf without really looking him in the eye. It's weird, almost like he's deferring to the animal. "Holden, we know she's hurt. Let us take her back home with us, so we can tend to both of you."

It takes a bit of coaxing, and Six-Three impresses me with his patience and calm in the presence of this wild animal, but to my surprise the wolf's body relaxes, and he backs out of the corner, giving the man room to get to me.

If I wasn't dying, I'd be really turned on right about now. Four smoking-hot naked men want to take me home with them? I can get with that. Not that "home" is where I need to be. I need to be in an ambulance, but Six-Three scoops me into his muscular arms and carries me out of the house to Eric's car.

"Hey! Matt! Grab the dead guy's keys, would ya?"

Five-Ten turns on his heels and trots back inside to get Eric's keys, and I ogle the view of his tight body receding into the house without shame. The flower tattoos curve up his hip onto his back. Nice.

I mean, I'm dying anyway. Who cares if I'm staring and drooling at my hallucinations?

Six-Three lays me across the back seat as soon as Five-Ten has the car unlocked, and he asks for my motorcycle keys. I give them to him with a shaking hand, and he tosses them to Five-Ten — er, Matt.

"Here. You can take her bike back to the house, I'll drive Red and Holden in the asshole's car, and Rick and Billy can run home."

Six-Two and Six-One — Rick and Billy, I guess — nod and disappear from my view.

Then Holden gets in the car.

I'd forgotten who Holden was already.

My body stiffens when the wolf crawls onto the back floorboard next to my seat. He rests his snout on my stomach and whines again, and I wish my hallucinations weren't naked. At least one of them needs to be armed with a tranquilizer gun to deal with this huge beast.

Six-Three rubs Holden's ear. "I know, bro. We're gonna get her home with us, and we'll get you both patched up." He turns to look at me. "You'll be okay. It looks like shit, but we've seen worse. Just hang tight. These back-woods roads are bumpy as hell, so I can't promise a smooth ride back here. Holden will help where he can, but he's hurt, too, so he can only do so much."

How the fuck is the wolf going to help keep me from bleeding to death? I want to ask, but a warm tingle flows through my body, and the next thing I know my lids become heavy, too heavy to keep open.

Chapter 3

I awaken amidst clouds and fluff and down and all the soft things, though something firm wraps around me, in stark contrast to the plush surroundings. I open my eyes to see two massive tattooed arms encircling me. Dozens of black-and-grey skulls of different sizes cover the arms, intertwined with plumes of wispy smoke. The effect is stunning, and I lie there entranced for several minutes before I realize a couple of things.

One: The owner of the arms, who is snuggled up behind me, has opted to wrap them around my chest.

Two: My chest, and I presume the rest of me, is buck-ass naked beneath those arms.

I shriek and burst free, tripping on the down comforter in my efforts to escape. I land hard on my knees next to the bed I'd been lying on, and a string of curses flies from my lips.

A deep, rumbling voice bellows in laughter from the bed. "Graceful *and* ladylike! Guess we got a package deal when we came to your rescue, huh?"

My cheeks burn as I grab the comforter and yank it off the bed to cover myself. Once I'm as decent as I'm going to get, I turn to face the man who was feeling me up in my sleep. I've got my mouth open to give him a piece of my "ladylike" mind about it, but when I get a good look at him, all I can manage is to gape in awe.

If I thought my hallucinations from earlier had been mega hotties, this guy — this guy is a fucking god.

Six-foot-five of pure sin wrapped in muscle and sinew and a six-pack that trails down into that sexy "V" that leads to …

… To a sheet that's draped over the part I am most curious about. Damnit.

"My eyes are up here, Red."

His snark reminds me that I'm angry with him. I glance up to his chiseled face and glare into his ocean-blue eyes, ready to reply with some snark of my own.

"My name's not Red, you jerk."

Wow. That's the best I can do? What the hell is wrong with me?

"Jerk, huh?" He sits up in one smooth motion and rests his elbows on his knees, none of which disturbs the sheet—much to my dismay. "I seem to recall getting stabbed in the act of saving your life. If that's jerk behavior, then I guess I'm guilty as charged."

"When did you save my life?"

"Last night."

That's right—I almost died last night. Was it really just last night? I peek under the blanket and see a bloodstained bandage on my flat stomach. I touch the area with gentle fingers, but nothing hurts. After a fall from the bed like I just took, I should be in agony with the cut that I had. I give the red spot on the bandage a good, solid poke, but still nothing. Curious, I peel away a corner of the tape, just enough to see how bad the wound underneath really is.

In place of the jagged cut from last night, there's nothing but an angry-looking raised pink scar.

How long was I out?

"Having fun under there?"

I wrap the comforter tighter around myself and

give the stranger on the bed my best indignant look. "Pervert."

He wiggles an eyebrow at me. "Is that such a bad thing?"

"Just how long have you been lying there feeling me up?"

He laughs again, and damn if he doesn't have the most adorable dimples underneath that sexy stubble. "It's been, what, five hours since we got back from the cabin? Six? I don't know; I didn't exactly have a watch on at the time, and even if I had, I was kind of busy with the huge-ass knife wound in my shoulder and all that." He rolls his shoulder as if testing it. "Judging by the healing, I'd say it was more like five hours ago. That about right, Geiger?"

Knife wound in his shoulder? Healing? Geiger? Is this guy on drugs?

A semi-familiar voice from behind me catches me off guard, and I jump when Six-Three answers Stranger with the Dimples. "Yeah, Holden, that's about right."

Jesus Christ, I didn't even know Six-Three—Geiger, I guess—was in the room. I must've been so distracted by waking up naked next to an equally-naked Holden that I didn't see or hear anyone else in here.

Wait a second … Holden? Wasn't that the wolf's name? Why the hell did they name the wolf after this guy? My brows furrow as I try to process the utter nonsense flitting about.

Holden doesn't seem to notice my confusion. "So, Geiger, Red here has informed me in no uncertain terms that her name is not, in fact, Red. She's neglected to tell me her name, though. Did you find any I.D. in her stuff? Y'know," he winks at me, "so I have something to call her that doesn't outright piss her off."

Geiger walks up and drops a pile of stuff on the floor next to me. When I look, my wallet's lying there, along with a pile of clothing and my moto boots. My wallet and boots are the only things I recognize. The rest is just a plain white t-shirt, some men's socks, and a pair of grey drawstring sweatpants.

"Where are my clothes?" I really don't want to dress like a bum in front of Holden and Geiger. My tank top was tight, my jeans fit like a glove, and that leather jacket was tailored to my curves. I don't mind that they saw me in *that* outfit, but even the comforter's better than some baggy-ass t-shirt and sweats.

Geiger answers. "You bled all over them. Matt's got the shirt and jeans in the washer right now to see if we can get them clean, but that jacket's a lost cause. Oh, and Holden, since you asked: Her license says her name's Cherry Duvall." Holden snorts, and I shoot him a glare as Geiger continues. "She's twenty-three, lives in a shitty apartment complex downtown, and, at least according to the DMV, is a real redhead. I was cleaning blood off me when Billy and Rick stripped her down and bandaged her, so I can't attest to the validity of her hair color. Let's see, what else? Five-seven, one thirty-five—"

"Hey! There's no need to announce my weight to the goddamn world!" For some reason, that bothers me more than Holden laughing at my name or Geiger debating the "validity" of my hair color.

"Don't worry your pretty little head, Cherry." Holden leans forward and flashes those dimples at me again, pairing them with a devilish white-toothed grin. "I'm going to tell you right now, however much you weigh is pretty goddamn perfect. Sits on you just right."

"Says the perv who was sleeping with his hands on my tits!"

He sits up and has the nerve to look offended. "Alpha healing magic requires constant physical contact, and with the way you thrash around in your sleep, it was the only way I could get you to hold still."

This time it's Geiger who chuckles, and fire burns in my cheeks again.

I'm pissed, and dimples or no, this guy's going to tell me what the hell he's talking about. "Look, Holden or whatever your name is, what the fuck is going on? Where am I? Why do you keep saying you helped save my life? I was pretty bad off, but I would've remembered a big guy like you in my grandma's bedroom. And who the fuck names their pet wolf after themselves?" I stop for a moment. "Hey, where is the other Holden—the wolf? He was hurt pretty bad..."

Tears well in my eyes as it hits me that the wolf, the creature that saved my life and offered me comfort on the car ride here, is missing. If Holden loves his wolf so damn much to name it after himself, then why isn't it here in the room with us? I look from Geiger to Human Holden and back again, and they exchange a weird glance.

"Oh, my God, not the wolf. Please tell me Eric didn't—"

Holden's lip curls up in a snarl at the mention of my ex. "That punk didn't kill the wolf. Don't worry; the wolf is fine."

I let out a sigh of relief. "Whew. Can I see him?"

There's the weird look between Geiger and Holden

again. Geiger clears his throat and averts his gaze. "It's up to you, Holden, but if you ask me you might as well. You've damn near admitted everything anyway."

Holden rolls his eyes, and I swear the dude growls under his breath. He stands up, discarding the sheet, and for a moment I forget Wolf Holden when I see the beast that Human Holden had hidden underneath the covers.

Oh, my!

I didn't even know you could get a tattoo there...

With a stretch that accentuates his exquisite muscles and a yawn that displays perfect rows of blinding white teeth, Holden works out whatever kinks he might have had from lying curled up next to me for so long. He sighs and runs a hand through his sandy hair. It's long, long enough for one of those cute man-buns, and part of me wants to just bury my hands in it. Those deep blue eyes meet mine, and I feel like I should follow Geiger's lead and look away, but I just can't.

"Get dressed. I'm not bringing the wolf out when you're sitting here in nothing but a blanket."

"Why should your pet wolf care if I'm dressed or not?"

This time I'm certain it's a growl I hear. "The wolf is not a fucking pet, Cherry. He's a wild animal, and the sooner you get that fact straight, the safer you'll be."

With that cryptic warning, Holden leaves the room. Geiger trails behind him and shuts the door, and I look at the pile of ugly clothing with dread. When I check the labels, I see that I've been gifted an extra-large size in both the V-neck t-shirt and the pants. Great.

I get into the clothes and pull the drawstrings on

the pants as tight as they'll go before tying them in a double-knotted bow. Thank God I've got hips, because otherwise I'd just be wearing the t-shirt—not that it's not long enough to count as a tunic on me, but I get the feeling Holden wouldn't be too thrilled if I strolled out there without any pants on.

I mean, he might be thrilled, but I wouldn't get to see Wolf Holden. I kinda owe that "wild animal" my life, after all, so I'll do as Human Holden says and wear the goddamn pants.

Now that I've got a little time to myself, I see that there's an adjoining bathroom inside the room I've been in. I go check myself out in the mirror and decide the outfit isn't too bad. I mean, the deep V in the extra-large shirt shows off my cleavage like nobody's business, and the pants sit just low enough on my hips that if I tie the bottom of the shirt in a little knot to gather it and cinch it up, I'm actually passable as cute. The bandage peeks out from under the knot, and since the cut is somehow mostly healed, I just pull the gauze and tape off and toss the bloody mess in the trash can. A quick twist and tuck of my long curls creates a messy bun, and I splash some water on my face to freshen up.

With my mass of hair out of the way, I have a better look at the scar on my neck. Is it just me, or is the thing thinner now, more faint? I'm not even sure I can see the suture holes anymore, and the redness has faded from violent red to a less-angry pink. Still noticeable, still a painful reminder of Eric's first attempt on my life, but no so obvious as to draw the stares that it has been the past week.

Yep, I'm almost passable as human again, almost back to Cheery Cherry.

Okay, so not the best moment to give that much of a shit about how I look, I know, but I'm in a house with no less than five hot, godlike guys — if my hazy blood-loss memory serves — and I am recently free of an abusive, controlling ex. I decide to give myself a pass on the ego.

After slipping on the huge socks and stepping into my moto boots, I open the door to the bedroom and come face-to-chest with Geiger, who must've been waiting for me. He's standing in the hallway with his arms crossed over his chest. "C'mon," he says, and he turns on his heel. "Holden's waiting, and neither the man nor the wolf is very patient."

I watch Geiger's tight ass in his jeans as he leads me down the hall. We pass a few doorways before coming to a massive great room with vaulted, open-framework ceilings, a huge brick fireplace on the far wall, and a scattering of bearskin rugs on the slick hardwood floors.

The whole gang's here. Holden commands the center of the room, bare-chested still but wearing a loose pair of linen pants, while Rick and Billy lounge on a couch, each with a beer in hand, and Matt stands off to the side, hands shoved in his pockets. The only one missing is the wolf.

Once again I marvel at the similarities between the five men. They're different for sure, but they're all tall and muscular, with sandy hair in various states of tousled perfection, and to a man they've all got chiseled jawlines and high cheekbones. Matt's the most clean-shaven of the bunch, as all the others have some degree of stubbly beard forming. Enough to play with, but not enough to get in the way.

"Are y'all brothers?" I don't mean to blurt it out, but the question has been burning in my mind.

Holden answers with a wry grin. "Quints, you could say."

I stop in my tracks, and my jaw gapes open. "Wait, you all have the same birthday?"

"That is, in general, what happens with quintuplets."

I stick my tongue out at Holden's sarcastic reply, and he dimples as he licks his lips and smiles wide. "Come. Have a seat." He gestures to a leather armchair next to him.

The vibe in the great room can best be described as jumbled; the boys' emotions read all over the place. Rick and Billy seem bemused, Matt's drawn brow gives an air of apprehension, and Geiger's so tense and serious that I wonder if he ever gives himself the freedom of relaxing.

Holden's harder to read. He starts pacing once I take my seat, cracking his knuckles and wringing his hands, and his lips are pressed in a thin line. His bare back sports a bright pink scar on the shoulder, almost a match to the scar on my stomach, and I wonder if he wasn't telling the truth when he said Eric stabbed him last night.

Did I pass out at some point and not realize it? I don't see how I could've missed seeing Holden in Granny Ethel's house.

"Are introductions needed?" he asks.

I shake my head. "Not really. I mean, last night is fuzzy, but I remember some of it. Matt's the one with the flower tattoos, I know, but I don't know which is which on the couch there. Is Rick the one with the wolf tat, or is it Billy?"

The man on the right side of the couch lifts his beer in salute. "Billy. That's me."

"Okay, so Rick's the one with the skull." I shrug my shoulders. "And I'm Cherry. Before any of you ask, yes, that's my real name. Mom was a bit of a modern-day hippie when she had me, and I guess when I was born I had cherry-red lips or something equally cheesy."

Holden stops pacing for a moment. "Your mom — Do we need to give her, or anybody, a call to let them know you're okay?"

I shake my head. "Nah. Mom and Dad quit talking to me a few years ago when I quit college in favor of bartending to support me and Eric. I don't even think I have their number anymore. Neither one of them approved of Eric." I lower my eyes and trace a seam on the arm of the chair with my fingertip. "I guess I should've listened to them."

Holden nods. "Okay. No phone calls then."

I frown as another detail pops into my head. "Hold up — Why, exactly, were the four of you naked in my grandma's house?" I turn to Holden. "What is with you guys and being naked?"

None of the brothers dignifies me with an answer.

"Where's the other Holden? You said if I put on this ridiculous outfit I could see him."

I watch four pairs of intense blue eyes take in my appearance. Geiger's standing behind the chair, so I don't know if he's ogling as well, but I find myself grateful for the mirror in the bathroom.

"You fill out Matt's clothes pretty well for a skinny girl, I'll give you that." Holden licks his lips again, and

I blush in spite of myself.

I decide to change the subject. "Wolf Holden —
Where is he?"

Human Holden steps in front of me and leans over
to rest his hands on the arms of the chair. I'm trapped
between the twin sets of smoking skulls, and when I
look into his eyes there's a smoldering intensity in them
that, not gonna lie, makes me a little wet between my
legs.

"You wanna see the wolf?"

"Yes, please." My voice comes out low and husky,
breathless even, and my heart pounds in my chest. I
should look away, something tells me I shouldn't be
making eye contact right now, but I just can't break
Holden's gaze.

He straightens and gestures at Geiger as he turns
his back on me. "Hold her down, dude. She's probably
gonna freak."

Geiger's hands come to rest on my shoulders, and I
shift to look at him. "What the hell am I going to freak
at? I've already seen the wolf; I'm not going to freak out
when he comes in here. Just let him in already."

Geiger avoids eye contact, his gaze locked on
Holden's back. He doesn't respond, but Holden does.

"The wolf's already here."

Chapter 4

Holden's voice sounds strange, almost strangled, and when I turn back around he's rolling his shoulders and cracking his neck like he's limbering up for a workout. He stretches his arms and inhales a deep breath.

I watch those delicious muscles and tendons of his ripple under his skin as he moves, and at first I appreciate the beauty there.

Then he stops moving, but the muscles don't.

The muscles keep rippling despite his stillness.

Then I hear a sharp cracking, and Holden's body spasms and twists, and I can't help the scream that surges forth.

His bare feet and chest and arms go from smooth to hairy right before my eyes, and the limbs shift and change. The feet elongate, and black claws spring from his toes and fingers. He throws his head back, and I see his jaw stretch until it's more of a snout. A familiar howl emits from his pulsing throat, and the linen pants rip clean off as his body continues to change.

My instinct is to try to bolt, but Geiger's grip tightens, and I'm forced to keep watching the excruciating transformation. It's like something out of a horror film, only the sound effects teams don't do justice to the crunch of bones shifting or the squelch of skin stretching.

"Just wait, Cherry. He's halfway there. Don't

panic."

Geiger's voice is calm. How can his voice be calm? Is he not seeing this? His brother is a fucking literal beast!

Holden drops to all fours and howls again as his sandy hair — shorter now, but covering his whole body — turns a greyish color. The sick cracking continues, and his back and limbs warp and compress until he's no longer even remotely human.

The wolf from last night stands at my feet, and I tremble at what I've just witnessed.

"What the *fuck* is going on?" I scream, and I thrash against Geiger's strong hands.

Wolf Holden turns around and sits on his haunches in front of me. His ears, now pointed and in a different spot on his head, perk up and rotate forward, and he cocks his massive, furry head as his tail — his motherfucking *tail* – thumps on the floor. It's the same look of curiosity I saw on the wolf in the forest when I was on the way to Granny's.

The same *exact* look.

Holy shitballs.

The wolf — Holden — whines and scoots closer. I try to back up, but I'm as far back as I can go, and Geiger's still got me pinned. I pull my legs up on the chair with me and tuck them under me in an attempt to make myself as small of a threat as possible, though I can't imagine I'd ever be any threat to the huge beast before me.

Holden whines again and nudges the scar on my stomach with his cold, wet nose. He licks the scar and rests his head on my lap with a huff. Soulful blue eyes — more crystal than ocean in this form — gaze into mine.

I remember the gaze, remember the tender nuzzle of the snout on my belly as I bled out in the back of Eric's car.

Even in this form, even as a "wild animal," Holden's only ever been gentle with me.

Some of my fear eases, and I reach a shaking hand to pet him, but I stop myself halfway there. Would tough, masculine Holden consider that an insult? I realize I don't know quite what to do. This wolf with his head in my lap is a wild animal, yes, but he's also a man, and even as I try to wrap my mind around that concept, I fall into those blue eyes. I decide to treat him like the man he is.

"M-may I?"

Holden's jaw gapes open, baring neat rows of sharp white teeth and fangs, and his tongue lolls out. He pants and thumps his tail on the floor again, and the image reminds me of a domestic dog that's feeling playful. I take these as good signs.

His fur is softer than any dog's fur I've ever petted. I run my fingers between his ears and down his neck, but I pause at the scar on his shoulder. Even transformed, Eric's wound remains.

The gravity of it all comes crashing into me. I almost died. Holden almost died protecting me, a woman whose name he didn't even know. We'll both likely bear these scars for the rest of our lives. Tears fill my eyes, and my shoulders shake beneath Geiger's hands. I wrap my arms around Holden's neck and sob into his thick pelt.

"I'm so sorry. Thank you so, so much, Holden. I owe you my life."

"What are we, chopped liver?"

Billy's voice startles me. I'd forgotten almost everyone else in the room; my world had kind of shrunk down to the wolf in my lap and the hands on my shoulders, but Billy, Rick, and Matt are all still here. I look up to take in my other rescuers. My mind still reels from it all, but the pieces are slowly coming together.

Five brothers. All born on the same day. All in peak physical health—and all naked in my grandma's house just moments after five wolves came to my rescue.

Holy shit.

Rick shoves Billy and frowns at him. "Dude, don't be a dick. She's been through a lot."

Billy takes another swig of his beer and belches. "Fucking had to run ten miles home through the woods after shifting twice, and Holden gets all the fucking glory. Stupid Alpha luck."

Holden growls in my arms but his tail still wags, so I think it's a good-natured growl.

Geiger's hands release my shoulders, and he perches on the arm of the chair. I'm surprised the thing doesn't tip over, but he's got some epic balance.

"You okay now?"

I nod and wipe my cheeks. "Yeah. I'm just— Fuck, shocked doesn't even begin to cover it."

"Any questions we can answer?"

"Probably a million." I laugh. "But for now, Billy's got a point. I should be thanking all of you. I mean, Holden killed Eric, but you all helped me, too. So thanks."

Geiger sighs. "I'd say you're welcome, but we're not done helping you yet. There's still the little matter of the bloodbath back at your grandma's cabin." He closes his eyes and rubs his forehead. "Now, we can go back and clean up some, but there's no way we're getting all of Holden's blood out of there. That's a problem, because we can't be letting a forensics team get hold of it, but at the same time, I know you probably want your grandma's body ... taken care of."

Shit. Granny Ethel. I can't believe I forgot about her. I mean, yeah, I had my own life to worry about, then I was surrounded by hot naked men, and then I was in Holden's arms, but still...

I bury my face in Holden's fur and groan. "I'm a terrible person."

A strong hand rubs the back of my neck. Geiger's closest, so I assume it's him, but when I look up, Matt's crouched next to the chair. "Hey. Don't say that."

My face crumples as my last fragile nerve shatters. "I forgot Granny Ethel! She's lying back there dead, and I forgot all about her."

Matt pulls me close, and the next thing I know arms surround me on all sides. Well, four pairs of arms and a wolf's shoulder. A veritable dogpile of men, all doing their damnedest to comfort me in my hysteria. As sobs wrack my body for what feels like the millionth time in a day, a warm buzz courses through me. It's similar to the buzz I felt at the cabin, but still distinct.

Within seconds the sobbing stops, and I'm able to breathe again. One by one, the brothers let go until it's just me, Matt, and Holden. I sniffle and sit up. "Shit. I'm a mess."

"No, you're not. You're traumatized. Now just take a minute to think about it. Do you want to go back there for her? Have us call the cops? Don't give me that look, Geiger; it's her right. Look, whatever you need, we're here, and we'll do whatever we can to take care of you." Matt squeezes my shoulder. "And if that means exposing ourselves to forensics, then that's what we'll do. You matter more than keeping some ages-old secret."

I stop to think on it. Granny Ethel was the one person who always sided with me, through thick and thin, through up and down, through the whole mess with Eric. She supported me, stupid choices and all, even when it cost her the relationship she had with her daughter.

Even when it cost her life.

"Burn it all."

I think I'm the most surprised of all of us at what I just said.

Matt just nods. "You got it." He nods at Billy and Rick, who get up and excuse themselves, and Geiger sighs. Holden seems content to keep his head in my lap.

"You hungry?"

I get the feeling that Matt's the sensitive one in the bunch. The pack? Anyway, a sandwich or omelet or something sounds amazing right about now, so I ask what they have. Matt says he'll fix me something, and he leaves me with Geiger and the wolf.

Geiger stands up and crosses his arms over his chest. "Not that I'm complaining, but are you sure you want us to burn the cabin down? There's still time for me to stop my brothers."

"I'm sure. Granny Ethel had just as few connections left in her life as I do. Mom and Dad didn't like her siding with me, so they haven't talked in years. No friends to speak of, no other family. A mysterious fire is as good a death as any, I suppose."

"Okay. What about the asshole?"

I blink a few times. "You mean Eric? Fuck him. He tried to kill me—twice." I point to the scar on my throat. Holden growls. "He's already burning in Hell, so let his body burn, too, and be done with him."

Geiger shakes his head. "No, that's not what I mean. Does he have any friends or family left? Anyone you can think of who might come after you now that he's dead?"

Oh. That. "Um, well, an older brother, Bishop. And he was kind of in a gang."

He raises a brow at me, and Holden cocks his head. "Kind of?"

I scratch the back of my neck and look down to avoid Geiger's piercing stare. "Well, I mean, they're not, like, an FBI-watchlist kind of gang. More like a bunch of gun-toting biker thugs."

"Gun-toting?"

Matt returns with a plate full of food. I smell peanut butter and jelly, potato chips, and something chocolate. My stomach rumbles as I take the bounty. Holden moves so I can balance the plate on my lap while I eat. "Okay," I say around mouthfuls of food, "so he wasn't, like, *in* the gang. I mean, they wouldn't let him go with them to certain places, and he wasn't allowed to carry a gun himself. So they might be an issue, they might not. Hard to say."

"What's the name of this not-gang?"

"Westside Mayhem."

Matt and Geiger share a look, and Holden woofs. Geiger nods, and the next thing I know he's out the door.

"Where's he going?"

"Off to do some research." Matt hands me a couple of drink options. The beer looks inviting, but I think I want to keep my wits about me, so I grab the bottled water instead. Matt opens the beer and drinks for himself.

Once I've finished the last of the cookies on the plate, I sit back and scratch between Holden's ears with an idle hand. "How long is he going to stay like this?"

Matt pulls another chair over and takes a seat across from me. "Probably a good hour. Shifting isn't the most comfortable of things to do, and he's still healing from that stab wound." He leans forward and gestures with his beer. "All that you saw just now is actually pretty damn painful most of the time. In an emergency, like last night, we can shift faster with less pain because of the adrenaline. No one's in danger right now, so his nerve endings are probably still a little bit on fire."

I jerk my hand back from Holden's head, and he whines. "Shit! Why didn't someone tell me that?"

With a laugh Matt reaches out and pets his brother. "Relax. If he didn't want you touching him, trust me, you wouldn't be touching him. Besides, Holden's the Alpha here, so he's got it a little easier than the rest of us. He can draw strength from the four of us to make the change easier, or to do cool stuff like healing the two of you."

"How many of you are there?"

"What, like here in this household, or are you talking on a global scale?"

Good point. "Here, I guess."

"Just the five of us. We had parents, of course, but a few years back they were killed in a nasty car crash. Freak accident on a stormy night kind of thing."

"I'm sorry." I lower my eyes and return to my therapeutic scratching of Holden's ears. "So… How does this pack thing work? You said Holden's the Alpha, and he mentioned something about it, too, but what are the rest of you? Do you just go down the Greek alphabet?"

Matt shakes his head. "Nah. Not quite, anyway. Geiger's our Beta, which is like a second-in-command, and I'm the Omega — I'm our calming influence, our balance in a way — but Rick and Billy are just pack members. They're the most submissive of us, but don't let that fool you; they can still be pains in the ass when they get in the mood. They'll follow Holden's orders over anything else, but they'll listen to Geiger, too, so long as it doesn't contradict with anything Holden says."

"Do you guys ever go into town and stuff?"

"Where the hell do you think we get the beer and peanut butter? Of course we go into town. We've all got jobs, too. Not that any of us really need to work; Mom and Dad made sure we were taken care of after they were gone. Mostly part-time stuff. Warehouse work, manual labor — things that make sense for big guys like us to do."

I chuckle at the thought of the five of them strolling into a nightclub. Panties would be dropping all over the place. I'd take any one of them, personally. Maybe more than one. I spent enough years tied to abusive, controlling Eric that I'm not sure when — or if — I'll be ready for another committed relationship again. "Do any of you have a girlfriend or wife or whatever?" I clamp a hand over my mouth, regretting the words the second they spewed from my mouth.

Damn. There I go, making things awkward. Go, Cherry.

This seems to take Matt off-guard. He sits back and lets out a low whistle and rakes a hand through his neatly-trimmed hair before he's able to answer me. "Uh, no. Dating is … difficult for us. I mean, can you imagine if you'd come across Holden here like this *before* we saved your life? Not that we can't control it— that whole full moon thing is a myth—but sometimes things happen, and next thing you know your wolf is ` front and center, whether it's physically like this or metaphorically.

"It's hard in other ways, too. Because so much of our personalities are tied to who and what we are in the pack hierarchy, we have to find someone who meshes with that personality. For instance, Holden here can't have someone who's too submissive or it'll fuck with his instinct to protect the pack, but at the same time a woman who's too dominant would make the wolf think its position as head of the pack is being threatened."

All this talk about submission and dominance reminds me of the kind of BDSM kink flick Eric loved to watch.

I wonder which I am: sub or dom. My first instinct is that I'm submissive, just because of all the shit I let Eric get away with. Then I remember that I didn't let him get away with *everything* he wanted, and I did fight back in the end. It almost cost me my life a couple of times, but I fought back.

"Can you tell by talking to a person if they're —
How did you put it? If you mesh."

"Shit." Matt turns bright red, surges to his feet, and
starts pacing. "This is really a conversation you should
be having with Holden."

"Oh." Guess whatever I am, it's not a good mesh
for an Omega. Too bad. Matt's cute — hell, they're all
cute — but he's got that boyish, sweet charm to him. I
imagine he'd be just as sweet in bed. I've never really
had "sweet" in bed before. "Sorry if I'm overstepping
here. I'm just curious."

"It's not that. It's just that, as Alpha, there are some
things Holden really should be answering."

A yawn sneaks up on me, and I cover my mouth
with the back of my hand. "Oh, fuck. Do you guys have
a guest room set up here? I just realized that I'm
exhausted, and I don't think I have the energy to drive
my bike back home right now. I need to lie down for a
few hours and get some real sleep."

Holden lifts his head and wags his tail. His ears
perk up, and he lets out a yip.

"Alone, Holden. I need to sleep alone for a while."

He whines and tucks his tail between his legs, ears
back, ducking his head down. Part of me wonders if his
behavior is similar to a domestic dog because of their
connection to wolves, or if he's doing it on purpose so
he can get his point across. How much of him is
Holden right now, and how much is the wolf?

"Yeah, we've got a guest room. C'mon; I'll show
you around."

Matt takes me on a quick tour that involves the
location of the kitchen, dining room, and hall
bathroom, where I guess the four non-Alpha brothers

share the facilities. The guest room turns out to be a different room than I woke up in, a few doors further down the hall and around a corner. I ask Matt why I wasn't put there to begin with.

"Holden was too badly injured last night. The Alpha wolf in him refused to let us take you anywhere but his room." He pats Holden's head and scratches behind his ears. "Don't worry, it's not like it sounds. You were hurt, too, and his wolf needed to protect you. Yes, this is our house, and it's perfectly safe here, but the wolf *needed* you in his territory, in his most familiar surroundings, to feel secure that he could take care of you."

I stretch and yawn again. "As long as neither he nor the wolf get any ideas about owning me, we'll all be fine. I've had enough controlling bullshit to last a lifetime."

Holden whines and huffs, and when he lies across the other side of the doorway to the guest room, his back is to the door.

Matt grins, and as soon as Holden lays his head down Matt plants a quick, silent kiss on my lips. When he pulls back there's a bright red flush to his face, making him all the more adorable. He puts a finger to his lips and winks at me before stepping over Holden and pulling the door shut.

My skin heats, and my heart pounds in my chest. I touch my lips, where the warmth of Matt's kiss still lingers.

He kissed me. One of the insanely hot brothers kissed me.

I stifle a girlish giggle, because I'm pretty sure Holden would hear it through the door, especially in wolf form. I have no doubt that he's parked himself there to guard me, and I'd put good money on him still being there when I wake.

A twinge of guilt creeps into my thoughts. Holden cares about me; that much is obvious. And despite my accusations when I woke up earlier, I have to admit he's been nothing but a gentleman to me. Even with his arms wrapped around my chest, his hands hadn't roamed or copped a feel that I was aware of.

I'm seconds away from opening the door to apologize when I stop myself. Despite the guilt I feel, I haven't done anything wrong.

It was just a kiss.

A sweet, tender kiss, stolen when his Alpha wasn't looking.

I shake my head to clear it of those thoughts and climb into the lush king-sized bed. Like Holden's bed, this one has only the softest of fabrics for bedding, and I fall asleep within moments of sinking my head into the plush down pillow.

Chapter 5

Sunlight streams through gauzy curtains, and disorientation slams into me. My apartment has blackout curtains on the small, barred windows. Why is the sun waking me up?

Memories of the past twelve hours come crashing back as I sit up on the edge of the huge bed, and I groan. I'm not sure I'm ready to face today. Granny Ethel's gone, burned to ashes by now, and as generous as the werewolf brothers have been, I doubt my welcome is indefinite. I'll have to go home at some point.

I look around the guest room, but then I remember that there's no guest bathroom inside. I'll have to venture out into the house and head down the hall to the brothers' bathroom, because after the ordeal I've had, my skin and hair feel slimy, greasy, and gross. I'm in desperate need of a shower.

As I rub the sleep from my eyes with one hand and reach for the doorknob with the other, I steel myself for a possible encounter with one of the brothers in my current rumpled state.

What I do not steel myself for, and thus scares the shit out of me when I open the door, is Holden's massive human form blocking the doorway. I shriek and jump back, and Rick and Billy burst out laughing from where they stand in the hallway behind him.

Holden grins. "Morning, Cherry."

I smile back and, without thinking, take in his appearance. My eyes glide downward, appreciating what they see. He's wearing a skintight t-shirt that matches the ocean blue of his human eyes, and he's got his thumbs hooked in the pockets of his equally tight jeans that hug every bulge and muscle. I jerk my gaze back to his eyes before I'm caught ogling, but I think I'm too late. Holden licks his lips and winks.

Busted. "Morning."

"How'd you sleep?"

"Okay, I guess. I could use a shower, though, and maybe some coffee after, if you have some." I feel silly for asking, but mornings and I do not get along unless there's coffee involved.

Those endless eyes bore into me, never leaving mine. "Rick, Billy, make yourselves useful and get some coffee started." Rick and Billy walk down the hall, still snickering at my startled reaction. "Anything else you need? I can get some more of Matt's clothes out of his room for you, if you'd like. Geiger isn't back from checking out your apartment yet, and I don't know if he'll be back before you're done washing up."

I frown, because it shouldn't take that long to check out the dump I live in. "Is everything okay?"

Holden shrugs his broad shoulders. His eyes change for a second, lightening to a softer blue, closer to the wolf's color, but they're back to normal so fast I wonder if I'm imagining things. "I don't sense any trouble. He's probably scoping the place out first, seeing if any of your asshole ex's buddies are around, before he goes inside. Geiger likes to play it safe."

I frown and tilt my head, curious. "You can sense him from here? Is it a wolf thing, or, like, a twin-slashquintuplet thing?"

"Good question. I've never thought about it, really. Maybe more wolf, I guess. Pack magic's a pretty complex thing, and Alpha magic even more so. I have to be able to know that my pack's okay, and where they are if they're not okay. I've heard that twins and other multiples have similar experiences to pack senses, but I don't think it's quite the same." He reaches out and ruffles my tangled hair. "Any other questions, now that I can talk again?"

My cheeks heat with the touch—and so do certain other parts of me. I avert my gaze to the side and clear my throat. "Maybe after my shower. I feel really gross right now."

He cocks his head, and his nostrils flare. "You smell great. But if a shower's more important right now, follow me. We've got spare washcloths and towels, even some extra toothbrushes. All the soap is unscented, though. We don't have anything fancy here. Bugs the shit out of us with our heightened senses."

"That makes sense, I guess." Although I'm not sure how I can smell "great" to Holden when I haven't showered since yesterday morning. I'm pretty sure the leftover sweat from the fear and utter panic in the cabin doesn't smell all that great, nor the general ick of not being clean. He's probably just being nice. "And yeah, I guess I'll take another t-shirt and pair of pants from Matt, if he's okay with that."

Darkness flashes across Holden's eyes, but it's brief. "He'll be okay with it." His gaze drifts downward. "From the looks of it, I'd better find something else with drawstrings. You've got some nice hips, but even as the smallest of us, Matt's clothes are enormous on you."

"Hey, you said Geiger was going to my apartment, right? Maybe he could bring back more than just one set of clothes—and maybe some underwear and socks or something? I feel weird wearing someone else's clothes all bare like this." A flush heats my cheeks. "I mean, well—"

Holden laughs and wraps a tattooed arm around my shoulders. "C'mon. We'll get you cleaned up and get some coffee in you, and maybe later you'll make sense."

The shared bathroom that the other four brothers use sits at the opposite end of the long hallway, and Holden keeps his arm on me all the way there. The drape remains casual and relaxed, but it creates a growing tension between us. My body reacts to the closeness and warmth; my muscles tighten, and my heart beats faster. The hallway feels warmer than before. I catch myself before I start fanning with my hand.

I know it's got nothing to do with the air conditioning. No amount of fanning will help.

At the door to the bathroom, Holden reaches in to turn on the light ahead of us, then slides his hand down to the small of my back, encouraging me to enter first. I walk in and gasp at the size of it, stopping just inside the doorway to take it all in.

"This should be the master bath! It's huge!"

When Matt had given me his tour the night before, the door to the bathroom had been closed. He hadn't given me a look inside, just directed me to where I needed to go if I needed to go. He hadn't shown me...*this*.

Holden just laughs. "Have you seen my brothers? They've all got to share this place, so it made sense when we built this place to make the hall bathroom bigger. I've got more than enough room for myself in the master."

The side walls have two sinks each, with a large beveled mirror over each sink. Bright fluorescent lights illuminate the room, and the chrome on the faucets shines. The back wall holds a huge shower with a frosted-glass door, and the toilet sits in an alcove to the side. White tiles with grey marbling line the floors and walls, matching the marble sinks and countertops. It's simple, yet elegant.

Holden squeezes past me and walks over to the wooden cabinet across from the toilet. His face disappears behind the door until as he digs around inside it for a moment, and he emerges with a triumphant toothy grin on his face. "There we go! New toothbrush, fresh, clean towels, and a couple washcloths for you." He sets his pile of treasure on one of the counters. "Best to put this stuff at Geiger's sink. He's the neatest of us. Soap and shampoo are all in the shower already, toothpaste should be in one of the drawers here. Feel free to snoop; the guys shouldn't have anything to hide."

"Um, what about Matt's clothes? You said you'd get me a change of clothes."

He raises his brows and looks taken aback. "Well, yeah. I'll go do that while you're in the shower and put them on the counter next to the towels for when you're done."

I look from the shower to Holden and back. The doors are frosted, sure, but still … "You're not going to grab them *before* I get in the shower?"

Holden blinks at me with a blank stare for a few seconds before realization sinks in. "Oh! Shit. That wasn't my intent, I swear." He scratches the back of his neck, and for the first time he averts his eyes and blushes. "No, I really was just going to drop the clothes off and leave, I promise. No peeking."

I sigh and put my hands on my hips. "Well, I mean, I guess it's not anything you didn't see last night, right?"

A pained look crosses his face. "I hope you don't think that I, or my wolf, claims ownership of you just because we spent a few hours in bed together. That really was to heal you, honest. I can't do that unless we're in close physical contact, because you're not a member of the pack."

I flush at the memory of my flippant words to Matt. "I'm sorry it came out like that. I wasn't trying to hurt your feelings or anything. It's just—Eric was controlling. Possessive. He thought that, since he was my first, he owned me. He got angry when I started dating again after breaking up with him, and that's when he came after me the first time and tried to slit my throat."

Holden's hand stretches towards the scar on my neck, but he stops himself. "May I?"

I nod and swallow past a sudden lump in my throat when he traces the scar with a soft touch. I do my best to hold still because his eyes have gone wolf-blue again, and something tells me that side of him is close to the surface when that happens.

The calloused fingers of his hand drift down to my collarbone and trace it to my shoulder. His other hand buries itself in my hair, and the next thing I know his full mouth is on mine. Everything is gentle, tender, but there's a power beneath the tenderness, a tension in Holden's body that's palpable as my hands brush against his broad chest. I lean into the kiss, and, despite my own efforts at showing restraint, moan against his mouth.

Without warning, Holden jerks back and lets me go. He walks to the door and grips the frame with white-knuckled hands. The fabric of his shirt strains against the tight muscles of his back as his shoulders rise and fall with heavy breathing.

"What's wrong?" I ask, a little breathless myself from that kiss.

Holden chuckles, but he doesn't turn back to look at me. When he speaks, his voice comes out gruff and husky. "The wolf— My wolf really wants you right now."

"Just the wolf?" It's more a question of curiosity than an attempt at flirting, but his back flexes when I say it, and his fingers dig into the wood of the door frame so hard it creaks.

He answers by growling a single word: "No."

A small part of my brain screams at me that I should be afraid, that I should run away, jump on my motorcycle, and never come back to this big house in the woods. I find myself planting my feet in place instead.

"If you and the wolf are in agreement, then what's wrong?"

Holden shakes his head. "Not now. Now I need a shower."

"Why? Because you smell like me now?" This is so

confusing. I don't know if I should be flattered that he wants me or insulted that he wants to wash me off him the second he's done kissing me.

"Let's just say you can feel free to use all the hot water you want, Cherry, because I won't need any."

With that he walks away, slamming the door behind him.

I stand there like an idiot for a solid minute before I realize he left me without a change of clothes for after my shower. I go to the closet he got my towels from and do a bit of searching, but aside from more towels, a couple bathrobes, and enough toilet paper for a worldwide pandemic, there's nothing. I pull out one of the bathrobes and set it next to the towels on the counter. It's not going to be much, but since it most likely belongs to one of the brothers, it'll be big enough on me to at least cover everything when I walk back down the long hallway to the guest room.

My shower takes longer than it should, in large part because of my fear of stinking in a house full of werewolves with hyper olfactory senses.

I step out and dry off, then slip into the bathrobe. It's almost too plush for a guy's robe, but the color is a dark grey, and the label lists a familiar men's clothing brand as the manufacturer. I tie the fuzzy belt as tight as it will go around my slim waist after making sure my chest is completely covered by the robe. The hem hangs down just below my knees, so I think I'm good to venture back to the guest room.

I bump smack into Geiger's chest when I exit the bathroom. That's what I get for piling all my towels and Matt's dirty clothes in my arms to carry to the laundry that I now realize I don't know the location of.

"Shit!"

He scoops up the laundry without missing a beat. "Here. Let me get that for you."

"Thanks. By the way, did Holden get hold of you before you left my apartment?"

"No. Was there something you needed? I can go back into town if there is."

Damn. So much for my underwear. "Nah. I just wanted more than one change of clothes, maybe some underwear and socks. It's not a huge deal."

He raises a brow at me as we walk side-by-side down the hall. "That's all? Well, then, it's a good thing I brought exactly that." Geiger winks and grins. It's not the toothy kind of grin that Holden gives, and he doesn't have the dimples his Alpha does, but it's a sexy grin all the same.

When I walk into the guest bedroom, I snort with laughter at the sight of half my belongings from my apartment, including all my dresser drawers—minus the dresser—stacked around the room. It looks like Geiger damn near cleaned me out. Laptop, tablet, toiletries, makeup bag, suitcases, no less than seven pairs of shoes. I'm surprised I don't see my fridge in the corner.

"What's so funny?" His head is cocked to the side like a confused puppy, which only serves to make me laugh harder.

"Dude, I'm surprised you weren't arrested for robbery!"

Geiger blinks and looks back and forth from me to my stuff. "I thought you'd want to be comfortable while you're here. I didn't know how long that would be, though—because I did indeed smell the biker gang members in the area around your apartment, so it's not safe to go back right now — and I didn't know what you'd need to be comfortable, so I just brought a bunch of it."

His cluelessness is just adorable. I lean against the door frame to steady myself while I catch my breath and take a closer look. "Oh, shit, you even brought tampons!" Seeing this brings forth a fresh wave of laughter.

"Well, I mean, if you're here more than a week or two you'll need them, so…"

This puts a halt to the laughing. "How the fuck do you know when my cycle will be?"

"You've ovulated recently. You're past the point of fertility, but I can still smell it. So that means another week, two at most, and you'll need them."

I put a hand to my forehead and groan. "Oh, shit, you guys can *smell* that? Ew."

He shrugs. "It's a natural thing. Nothing to be embarrassed about. Most of us wolves like the scent. Reminds us of sex."

That stops me cold. I straighten and look at Geiger with narrowed eyes. "My smell reminds you of sex? Like, how much does it make you think of sex? Enough to, say, turn you — or your wolf — on?" I think back on Holden earlier. "Enough to make you need a cold shower?"

"What? No. It takes more than the smell of ovulation to turn us on that much. But the scent is something we, or the wolf parts of us, I guess, associate with sex, so we find it pleasant." His nostrils flare, and he inhales a deep breath. "For instance, you smell like our soap and shampoo, but you also smell like recent arousal. That's attractive to us."

"I smell like ... Oh, shit!" I bury my face in my hands to hide the red-hot blush spreading through my skin. "You're kidding me! I scrubbed and scrubbed in that damn shower."

"Am I upsetting you?"

"No," I mumble through my hands. "You're just very, very honest, Geiger. It's refreshing, if not a little humiliating."

He puts a hand on my back and starts rubbing in a small circle. "I'm sorry. That wasn't my intent at all. I just tend to be more, let's say, analytical than my brothers. Sometimes I get carried away with the facts and forget about the feelings."

"It's okay."

"Do you need me to help you put away your things?"

"No, that's okay. I've got it. I think I need a few minutes alone, anyway."

The circling hand pauses at my lower back, just long enough that I worry he's going to smell arousal on me again. If he can, he doesn't mention it. Instead, he pulls me close for a half hug and kisses my forehead. "Things will be strange and confusing for a few days, I imagine, for all of us. We're used to the life we live by ourselves, so we forget what's normal and what's unusual for regular humans. Be patient with us. It's not like any of us have never dated, but we're not accustomed to a woman hanging around, especially not one as attractive as you. Give us some time." With that, he leaves and disappears around the corner of the hall.

Great. So three out of five wolves already know I'm hot for them just by smell, and all three, it seems, are attracted to me as well. I almost dread going to the kitchen for the coffee that Rick and Billy were brewing up for me. Hell, it's probably cold by now. I'll have to heat it up.

I throw on a tasteful pair of underwear — not a thong or G-string, but still something nice — an older pair of worn jeans, and a black babydoll tee with a pair of cherries on it that hugs probably more than I should be letting my clothes hug me right now. I wrestle my wet curls into a loose braid down my back, and after some internal debate I decide to forgo any makeup, lotion, or perfumes. I remember what Holden said about scented stuff, and I don't have anything that's subtle. If it smells strong to me, it's going to smell even stronger to them.

On the other hand, if it overpowers the scents of arousal and recent ovulation, …

No, better not.

A pair of low-heeled ankle boots finishes my look, and I head for the smell of coffee. I remember where to find the kitchen from my tour with Matt last night, so I make a beeline for the aromatic beverage.

Chapter 6

I walk into the kitchen to the sounds of literal howls and wolf whistles. Billy and Rick both lean against the counter and cheer me when I wander in. Judging by the wide grins and twin winks, they approve of the outfit. Both men are shirtless, and they've got dirt smeared all over them. I wonder what dirty, sweaty activity they've been up to today. "Hey, guys. Coffee ready?"

Rick grabs the pot and pulls a mug out of a cupboard behind him. "Yep. We even waited until the shower stopped so it would still be hot for you."

"Speaking of hot for you," Billy's grin widens, and he wiggles his eyebrows, "if you want some cream, ..."

Rick smacks him upside the head. "Dude! What the hell is wrong with you?"

"What? C'mon, surely you smell it, Rick."

Grateful for the earlier conversation with Geiger and my new understanding of what they're talking about, I manage to brush it off with a roll of my eyes and a choice finger in Billy's direction. "Coffee. Black. Now."

Rick laughs, but Billy's face falls. Rick hands me a full mug with a low, courtly bow. "Mad respect, Cherry. Mad respect." When he straightens, his bare nipples are hard little nubs on his chiseled, tattooed chest. The flames on the skull move with his breathing, creating a hypnotic effect.

I take a sip and breathe a sigh of relief as the bitter caffeinated elixir works its way to my stomach. "Oh, I don't know about that. I mean, if I was any kind of dominant personality, Eric wouldn't have had me on such a short leash when we dated." Another sip, and more of the tension built up from the past twelve hours melts off my shoulders. I roll the aching muscles and joints with a soft moan. "He used to have his brother and his biker buddies keep tabs on me. If he couldn't be at the bar while I worked, I guarantee you one of the others was there, watching my every move. God forbid if I even so much as smiled at one of the patrons."

Both brothers bristle at the mention of my dead ex, but Billy's face lights up moments later. "Hey! Hurry up and finish your coffee. We have a surprise for you."

I hold up an index finger while I take yet another sip, drawing it out as my lids hood my eyes. With a sigh and a smile, I swallow the sip and lick my lips. "Never hurry coffee unless you're late for work."

Billy groans, a deep, feral sound. "Are you sure you're not an Alpha?"

A distant part of me wonders if I'm playing with fire here. I'm attracted to all five brothers, no doubt about it, but I know precious little about werewolves and their mating-slash-dating protocols. Is it wrong to kiss Matt and Holden yet still want to grind against serious Geiger or have a little fun with Rick or Billy — or both?

Each man has a different personality, a different draw that pulls me towards them, and I find myself in a position where, at least for the time being, I can't make up my mind which one or ones I want.

I kinda want to have a little taste of each before I

have to decide.

I finish my coffee and set the mug down with a shake of my head. Dangerous game or not, I'm safer here than back home at my apartment. Here they may be part animal, but Eric's brother and his biker pals share a level of cruelty and venom that only pure humankind is capable of. Wolves have honor and loyalty. Those assholes? All they've got are guns and compensation issues.

Having seen each of the brothers naked, I know that none of them have anything to compensate for.

"All right, now I am sufficiently caffeinated. Billy, what's this surprise you mentioned?"

Billy grabs my arm with a devilish grin and pulls me to the outer door of the kitchen, which looks like it leads to a wooded area behind the house. Rick shoves his hands in his pockets and follows behind us.

We walk for about ten minutes, heading deeper and deeper into the forest that surrounds the brothers' sprawling home. A narrow path trails through the trees with so many twists and winds that I'm grateful for Rick and Billy's heightened senses. Even if I get lost out here, they probably could find our way back blindfolded.

A small clearing opens before us, and I stop in my tracks. The small, round space is well-kept, with smooth, trimmed grass and a smattering of wildflowers that seem to be cultivated rather than wild.

My eyes are drawn to a rectangular mound of freshly-disturbed dirt with a wobbly wooden cross at one end. It's incongruous with the rest of the landscaping, and I'm confused until I recognize the name "Ethel" painted on the cross. I blink away tears as

I allow myself to scan the rest of the clearing, my stunned brain finally taking in two neat rows of smooth, polished marble headstones. Five headstones total, not counting Granny Ethel's hasty marker.

Dear God, these boys not only took care of Granny's home for me, they also took the time to bring her body here and inter it with their own family members.

They gave Granny Ethel a proper burial.

I take a few shaky steps to the foot of the grave and drop to my knees. Deep, racking sobs burst forth from deep inside, and I place my hands on the dirt as the tears flow free.

It's more than Mom and Dad would have done; if we'd reported the murder to the police, they would've had Granny cremated and flushed the ashes. My parents are just that spiteful. Granny took my side over theirs, and they'd never let that go, not even after Granny's death. Hell, they'd probably blame her for her own murder, saying it was her fault for not shunning me the way they did.

Two pairs of muscular arms wrap around me, and I bawl into Rick and Billy until all my tears have run out.

When the last hiccupping sobs have passed, Billy presses his forehead against mine. "It's not much, and I promise we'll get her a real headstone, but at least now you'll have a place to visit her."

Rick nuzzles my neck on the other side of me. "And it doesn't matter whether you stay or not. You can always come visit, any time."

We sit together in the grass like that until my stomach rumbles, and laughter bubbles from my throat. "Shit. I guess it's lunch time. I forgot to grab something to snack on back in the kitchen."

The three of us walk back hand in hand, and I'm grateful for the warmth of their hands in mine. It's kind of nice, having people who give a shit. People who care. People like Matt, who takes the time to explain things to me. People like Holden, who shows restraint out of respect. People like Geiger, who hauls half my shit all the way here for me. People like Rick and Billy, who think of things I never would have.

I almost wish I could stay forever.

Holden waits on the back porch when we emerge from the woods, and, judging by the tension in the corded muscles of his arms crossed over his chest and the wolf-blue glare, at least one of us is in trouble, if not all three.

Rick and Billy release my hands and look at the ground with slumped shoulders.

I wipe my palms, which have begun to sweat, on the seat of my jeans, and I realize the mistake I made the second I see Holden's nostrils flare. I probably shouldn't be drawing attention to my ass when I've just spent an hour alone in the woods with his brothers, regardless of the innocent nature of it all. Geiger could smell my attraction to Holden on me *after* I scrubbed in the shower, and I'm sure the scent is fresher now after the closeness with Geiger and the other two flirting with me in the kitchen.

Like a coward, I let Holden's brothers ascend the porch steps ahead of me. They pause next to him, and, without breaking his gaze, Holden tells them to wait for us in the great room.

Shit.

Heat radiates off Holden as I stop at the top of the

stairs. His breathing comes fast and shallow. He doesn't move, but at the same time his entire body trembles with restrained emotion.

Problem is, I don't know yet how to tell which emotion he's trying to restrain more.

I know I should look away from those crystal blue eyes. I shouldn't keep eye contact when he's this pissed. I remember hearing something in a documentary about wolves, something about how direct eye contact is considered a challenge. I don't want to challenge Holden, not in this state, but I can't bring myself to avert my eyes.

"There's dirt on your knees." The words come out in a low, rumbling growl.

Oh, shit. Oh, *fuck*. Does he think —

"Your brothers brought Granny Ethel's body back. They buried her with your family in the woods. I was just saying goodbye." His pupils dilate, and I scramble for words that won't make him angrier. "Nothing happened, Holden, I swear."

More rapid breathing. Bigger pupils. Another growl.

My instincts scream at me to step back, to get out of his reach, to get the hell out of his territory before he includes me as part of it. My hormones, on the other hand, argue that we should stay put and growl back. I've never been this horny around a guy who's this angry. When Eric got pissed, I got scared. Terrified, panicked, yes, but turned on? Definitely not.

I want to grab his hand, drag him to the woods, shove him against a tree, and ravage him. I want to jump his massive bones *right fucking now*, and if I'm being honest with myself, that's more frightening than

Holden himself.

I don't know how long the standoff lasts. It feels like forever, but it can't be more than a minute or two before Holden finally looks away and closes his eyes. "I know nothing happened. I don't have a right to know or care if anything did happen, I guess." He opens his eyes again, and they're almost back to his darker human blue shade. The man is back in control—for now. "You, Cherry, are one dangerous lady to have around."

"Does that mean you're going to make me leave?" Oh, God, I hope not. I'm not ready to leave this place.

He shakes his head and lets out a shuddering sigh. His body relaxes, and he runs a hand through his hair. "No. Not now, anyway. We took you in to protect you, and we're not going to just throw you back out to the wolves, so to speak. Until it's safe for you to go back, you can stay. If you want to."

"I want to." The words barely make it out of my mouth. Hell, if Holden doesn't have supernatural wolf hearing on top of the sense of smell, he probably can't hear what I just said.

I guess he's got that wolf hearing, though, because he nods and steps aside so I can get past. I walk into the house feeling like I've got my tail between my legs, and when I get to the great room where Holden's four brothers wait for us, I almost wish I *had* a tail to shove between my legs. My shame should be visible enough in my slumped shoulders and ducked head, if not in my fucking scent, but I feel kind of left out in this group that has this whole separate language to use to express themselves.

I take a seat in a chair off to the side, rather than the

open spot on the couch between Rick and Billy. I get the feeling I need to distance myself from the other men for a little while.

To my relief, Holden pulls the door shut behind him with a gentle hand, so it doesn't slam. I'll take that as a good sign that I'm not about to get my ass handed to me in front of everyone.

Holden stands in the center of the room and takes a deep breath. He makes eye contact with each of us in turn, and everyone else looks away. Not me. I'm the dumbass who makes silent challenges. "Guys, we have a problem."

Chapter 7

Here it comes. I guess I'm getting my ass handed to me after all.

"Rick, Billy, you did a decent job of covering up what happened in Cherry's grandma's cabin, but not good enough it seems. The arson's all over the news, as well as Eric's charred and —" he makes air quotes with his fingers " —mutilated body."

"Shit." Billy cringes and runs his hands through his hair.

"Yeah. I don't think there will be enough left for forensics to lead to us directly, but there will be questions, that's for sure. Geiger got rid of Eric's car earlier today, but people are still going to wonder where Ethel went, why Eric was there, and where Cherry is. In fact, they're looking for Cherry specifically." He turns to me. "You're a person of interest in the case. Your helmet was found at the cabin, so they know you were there."

My heart thumps hard in my chest as the implications sink in. If my body isn't found, the cops will assume I did it. I'd get off on self-defense — I have the scars to prove that Eric tried to kill me more than once — but how can I explain away Eric's shredded throat, Granny Ethel's disappearance, or how I miraculously survived the deep cut in my stomach without needing a hospital?

Then there's the not-so-small matter of Eric's

brother and the biker gang. At least one of the two is going to want revenge, if not both — Bishop for the obvious reasons, the biker gang because they can't let someone get off scot free with killing one of their own, no matter how fringy Eric was.

I am in deep, deep shit. The brothers, too, if it gets out that they helped me. This whole fucking mess is my fault.

"Cherry?"

I jump at the sound of my name. The brothers all stare at me, and Holden's brows are drawn together. He takes a step towards me. "Are you okay?"

I let out a dry, mirthless chuckle. "Oh, sure. I'm about to be wanted for murder, probably the arson too, and I'm sure I've got more than a few people outside the law who are going to want to see me dead for it all. And, in the process, I've endangered you sweet guys with my stupid decisions. I'm great."

Rather than getting angry for my snark, Holden's face softens. He crosses the room and sits on his heels next to my chair, taking my hands in his. "We will *not* let them hurt you. And don't worry about us. This wouldn't be the first time we've been in trouble, and I'm sure it won't be the last."

My gaze drops to our hands. His dwarf mine in comparison, but there's something about the way they envelope my slender fingers that comforts me and slows my panic. My heart, however, surges at the touch, and my breath comes quicker.

Much as I would love to stay like this forever, I have to get out of this room. Ever since Geiger clued me in to their sensory secret, my awareness of my body's responses to their presence has been heightened, and I worry that something will happen to make the brothers fight if I can't get my hormones in check. I swallow past a hard lump in my throat. "Can I have lunch in my room, please? A sandwich and some chips like last night would be fine. I'm just a little worn out, I guess."

"Sure. What would you like to drink?" He chuckles and strokes my cheek. "You probably want a beer right about now, if not something stronger."

"No, actually, water's fine. And," I look around the room, "whispering is kind of pointless around you guys, isn't it?"

Another smooth, deep laugh. Damnit. Stop being charming. "Yes. There's no way you could whisper low enough that I'd be the only who hears you."

Sigh. "Okay, then, I'll just say it: Could you be the one who brings my lunch to me, please, Holden?"

I regret the words as soon as they're out of my mouth, but it's too late now. Matt's face falls, the two brothers on the couch grow tense, and even Geiger's jaw works as he grinds his teeth so loud I can hear it across the room.

Fuck. They think I've made some kind of final decision, some choice.

I have, but not the kind of choice they think I made.

I stand up with a groan and do my best not to let my hips sway as I walk away. The last thing I need to do is spark any fires in that powder keg of a great room with my exit.

A harsh, whispered "fucking tease" drifts down the hall behind me, and tears sting my eyes.

When I get to the guest room, I slam the door behind me and start throwing random shit into my suitcases. I can't see with how hard I'm crying, so I could be packing useless stuff. I could be packing the brothers' guest items. I don't care at this point. I made a mistake. I need to go. I have to get out before I do any more damage.

A few minutes later a knock on the door scares the shit out of me, and I scream "What the fuck do you want?" without thinking.

There's a long pause, after which Holden's voice answers me. "Um, I thought *you* wanted me to bring you lunch, so I did."

"Shit!" I grab the closest item of clothing and wipe my face as I try to control the sudden attack of hiccups that spasm in my chest. Each hiccup brings fresh physical pain to compete with the emotional pain I feel, and oddly enough, I welcome it. I clench my hands into fists with my nails digging into my palms to bring more real hurt to detract from the heartache. "Come i-*hic*-in."

I keep my back to the door when Holden enters. He sets the lunch tray in my line of sight on the bed but otherwise makes no attempt to approach me. The door shuts a moment later, and I throw myself face-down on the bed. Fresh sobs wrack my body. I scream into the covers.

Holden's hand touches my back, and I sit up with a shriek.

"Fuck! I thought you left!"

He backs up and holds his hands up, palms out, his crystalline eyes wide. "I was just closing the door to give us some privacy. You are clearly upset about something, more than just the whole Eric shitshow, and I wanted to give you a chance to talk with less risk of the others listening in."

"Is there anywhere in this house they won't hear everything anyway?"

"We did some pretty good soundproofing when we built this place. Five single guys in one house—and with our senses? None of us really wants to hear any of the others having sex with a date."

I grab a pillow, cover my puffy face, and lie on my back. "What is with you guys and sex? You're all on, like, twenty-four seven."

Holden laughs, and I feel his weight sink into the bed next to me. I notice that he doesn't actually sit so he's touching me, but enough heat still radiates off his massive frame that I sense the shift in temperature. "Us? Cherry, I've smelled your heat at least half a dozen times since you woke up in my bed. You don't get to call us out on being horny when you're just as bad."

"Not my fault you're all so damn hot. And nice. Fuck, why do you all have to be both?"

Something presses into my stomach, something small, and I realize Holden has set my sandwich there. "Eat. Breathe. Finish crying first, if you have to. I'll sit here all day, and I promise I won't do anything you don't want me to—*really* want me to—unless you give me the green light. No pressure. Deal?"

I sniffle into the pillow and nod.

"Cool."

The bed moves, and when I peek out from under the pillow Holden's reclined against the headboard, with an arm slung across one raised knee and the other leg hanging off the edge of the bed. His posture screams ease and relaxation, but even when he's just chilling, he's hot.

With a huff I flex my abs and sit up, discarding the pillow and catching the sandwich before it falls on the floor and ruins my lunch. I take small nibbles at first, but once I've calmed down from my initial hysteria my stomach reminds me that I haven't eaten all day, and I devour the rest. After I finish the chips and cookies, I wash it all down in one long dredge from the water bottle. A few drops slide down my chin and my neck, and I don't miss the color change in Holden's hooded eyes when I wipe it off, particularly when my hand brushes against the scar over my jugular.

"It doesn't hurt anymore, you know, not since you healed me. And he's dead, anyway, so you don't need to bristle every time I touch it."

"I can't help it. You were hurt, and even though I didn't know you at the time, it angers my wolf that I couldn't do anything to stop it."

Something about his phrasing sparks a question. "Why do you and the others talk about the wolf side of you like it's a separate entity? Is it like multiple personalities or something? Are you and Wolf Holden really two entirely different beings, or is it just something you say to dumb it down for us normies?"

"That's … complicated. I mean, the wolf and I are the same, but that part of me has its own control over my body and my reactions to things. There's a definite disconnect sometimes, even though we're both *me*. I've noticed you watching my eyes a lot, so you've probably picked up on the times when the wolf starts to come to the surface. If my eyes change when I'm angry or in response to some other negative situation, like when you were hurt and in danger, it's extremely hard to keep the wolf in the background." He gives me a pointed look. "If my eyes change when I'm angry, it's a really, *really* dumb idea to stare right the fuck into them like you do."

This time, I'm smart enough to look away, even though his eyes are back to human blue. "I know. I'm not sure why I do that."

Holden chuckles and reaches out to tuck a stray lock of hair behind my ear. "I have a theory on that, but for now just try to remember."

"Okay."

"Any other questions? I promise to be as open as I can, within reason. If it's something personal about one of my brothers, I'll just tell you to ask them. Just because I'm the Alpha doesn't mean I have the right to go spilling their secrets."

"Fair." I scoot back until I'm leaning against the headboard next to Holden, but I take care not to brush up against him. "Is that why Matt deferred to you on the subject of werewolves dating?"

He stretches an arm around my shoulders and, with a gentle tug, pulls me close. He keeps his hand resting on my shoulder, though his thumb rubs back and forth against the fabric of my shirt. It's soothing, almost hypnotic. "Yes and no. He wasn't really trying to hide any secrets I may or may not have, but as Alpha, it's kind of tradition that I explain most of the whole schtick when we let a human see us for who we are. That, and I think he felt a bit awkward about it. He's in a unique position in the pack—not dominant, not submissive, but a melding of the two that helps keep us in balance. You have enough dominance in your personality that I think maybe he wasn't sure of his place in the pack hierarchy when it comes to you."

"Why do you guys keep saying I might be dominant? With the way Eric fucking walked over me and controlled me when we were dating, and even after we broke up, I'd have pegged myself as a sub, not a dom."

Holden stifles a snort with his free hand. His dimples pop with his amusement. "Okay, I'm going to stop you right there. One: you would literally be incapable of looking my wolf in the eye if you were at all as submissive as you're trying to make yourself out to be. Two: please don't call it 'dom' and 'sub.' This is a wolf shifter pack, a family, not a BDSM kink club."

I allow myself the freedom to giggle at that, and I relax a little more against Holden's frame, resting my head on his broad shoulder. "You just said 'wolf shifter.' Do you guys not call yourselves werewolves? I mean, that's what you are, isn't it?"

"Not really. We don't change at the full moon, we weren't bitten, and we can't transmit our shifter abilities with a bite. Shifters are born this way; werewolves are, to my knowledge, either cursed or diseased."

"Oh." I feel a little chagrined at being corrected, but I guess I should give myself a break for my ignorance. It's not like the distinction between wolf shifters and werewolves is common knowledge or anything. "So you've been able to shift from human to wolf and back since you were a kid?"

"A baby, actually, though at that age it's more awkward and not nearly as smooth of a transition as you witnessed last night. Oftentimes, shifter infants will shift a limb on accident and scream for their mother or their Alpha, who will have to use pack magic to either finish or revert the change until the kid's old enough to handle it."

"Shit! You mean you can get stuck?"

He heaves a sigh and rests his chin on my head. "Only when we're really young. You learn real fast how to either finish the change or stop it, or else — "

"Or else what?"

"Or else you live in agony."

Wow. That's some heavy shit for little kids, for babies to have to deal with. I can't even imagine. "But you were already changed last night when I was driving down the road, weren't you? That was you I saw, wasn't it?"

Holden nods. "Yep. Sometimes we go out as a pack — a family outing, if you will — and roam around in wolf form. I caught wind of something that didn't smell right, a mixture of blood and death and rage, and I was headed to your granny's house to investigate when you drove by. That's how we were able to show up in time; we were already in the area."

"I'm glad you were. I don't think Eric intended for me to live through that encounter."

A low growl rumbles through Holden's chest.

"Hey, now, none of that. Just be proud that you killed the bastard."

"Oh, I am," his voice comes out hoarse and gravelly, "but that's not going to stop me from hating the asshole every time I hear you mention him."

"Speaking of hating people, I think I pissed off at least a couple of your brothers just now, when I asked you to bring me lunch."

Holden's grip on my shoulder tightens. "What do

you mean?"

"One of the others, I think Rick or Billy, called me a tease just now, when I left the room to come in here. Well, the specific term was 'fucking tease.' I'm a little too mortified to go back out there, but when we're done talking, do you think you could maybe talk to them? I don't want any of you to think I've been trying to tease. I'm not like that, I promise. I'm just kinda confused."

He squeezes my shoulder, and his hand dips a little lower. He's now touching the bare skin on my arm with that hypnotic thumb, and I want to say how good that feels, how calming—but I'm afraid to be taken the wrong way.

I'm also afraid to be taken the right way.

"I would, Cherry, but it's really not my place to. That's something you have to, *ahem*, dom up and do yourself."

Damn. "Oh. Okay."

We sit in silence for several minutes before I work up the nerve to ask my next question.

"If I'm going to stay here, I'll have to make a decision, won't I?"

I'm vague on purpose, but judging by his deep, drawn-out sigh, Holden knows what I mean. "I *should* say 'yes.' I should tell you to choose now, before the fur and fangs start flying. But I'm not going to. Not just yet. You've been thrown into an impossible situation, and I guess us wolves are to blame for some of it, especially with our behavior. I know I didn't do myself any favors with my actions in the bathroom this morning. I realized later that I sent just about the most mixed signals I possibly could, and I'm sorry for that."

I stretch to kiss his cheek. "Don't ever apologize for showing restraint, especially not when I was in a really vulnerable place. I actually appreciate it."

Holden closes his eyes and lets out a low growl, and his body tenses. "You're making it harder to show that restraint, Cherry. Tread lightly; the wolf is close."

"Is that a warning?"

"It might have to be, if you keep this up."

Feeling emboldened by his comments on my dominance, I put a hand on his toned inner thigh. "What if I want what the wolf wants?" My voice surprises even me with its breathiness.

"Cherry, if you don't stop right now, no cold shower is going to help me this time. The wolf will come out, and he's wild; he might not be gentle after waiting so long for this."

His wording makes me freeze. "Will he hurt me?"

"No ... never."

That's all I need to hear. I slide my hand along Holden's hip, under his shirt, and up his stomach to caress his broad chest. I let myself explore the corded power of his muscles, and while my hand explores, I shift until I can reach the crook of his neck with my mouth. I nibble and lick and nip, light touches, but from the growing bulge in his jeans, I'm achieving the desired effect.

"Cherry?" Holden's voice is rough with emotion.

"Mm-hmm?" I don't stop what I'm doing.

"Is this the green light?"

In one smooth motion I swing a leg over his lap so I'm straddling his crotch. I take his face in my hands and wait for him to open his eyes, eyes I know are that gorgeous crystalline blue.

His lids flutter open, and I issue my challenge by boring my green eyes into his. "Go."

Chapter 8

The next growl from Holden's throat is playful, and his dimples appear as he grins that sexy, toothy grin of his. He takes hold of my hips and, with a quick thrust of his pelvis, grinds his bulge against the crotch of my jeans.

Despite the fact that we're both still fully clothed, the motion makes me gasp. I roll my hips to return the favor, and Holden throws his head back against the headboard as I ride him through our jeans. "That feels fucking amazing," he groans through gritted teeth. "I can hardly wait to feel you do that while I'm inside you."

"Patience, Alpha." I lean in and plant a soft kiss on his generous mouth.

My intent is to take my time, to savor this, but Holden's wolf wants more. He buries a hand in my braid and holds me to him, his tongue probing past my lips to caress my teeth while his other hand fumbles with the buttons on his fly.

Once his erection is freed, I pull back from his mouth with a final nip of his lip before I start making my way to my goal. I wrap a hand around his shaft and stroke his cock while I kiss, lick, and nibble his neck and throat. He whines, a pleading sound, and pushes into my hand. The velvety skin is a stark contrast to the hardness underneath.

With my other hand, I push his shirt up to give me

access to his bare chest. I continue my descent, alternately biting and planting soft kisses as I go, pausing only to suck on each hard nipple before trailing down his ribs and stomach.

The whole time, Holden makes these animalistic noises that drive me wild. The growls, whines, whimpers, and groans all turn me on even more.

When I lick the salty drop of precum from the tip and take him into my mouth, he shudders and sighs. His hand rests on my head, fingers threading into my hair, but to my relief he doesn't try to guide or force my head. I always hated when Eric did that.

Thoughts of my dead ex bring a growl of my own to my throat, and I push them back to focus on the task at hand.

"Oh, God, Cherry, I love how that feels."

I look up, but his head is still leaned back. His Adam's apple bobs as he swallows hard, and I suck harder, pull him farther into my throat. My hand continues to pump the bottom of his thick shaft, rubbing the flame tattoos as I take him as far as I can without gagging. Holden's cock is just as huge as the rest of him, so I can't get it all, but once I've got him as deep as I can I growl again.

His fingers tighten in my hair, but still he refrains from pushing. "Oh, Cherry…"

My head bobs as I suck and lick his cock, and I taste more salt at the back of my throat. He throbs inside my mouth, and just before he explodes, Holden grabs my shoulders and pulls me off. My lips make a wet popping sound when they release him, and I look up at him, confused.

"Take your clothes off." His voice is thick and raw.

"My turn."

I grin and sit up to pull my shirt off over my head. Before I've even got it all the way off, Holden wraps his arms around me and latches onto my breast with his mouth, licking and sucking my hard nipple. The sensations are off-the-charts good, and I arch my back and moan. When Holden grips my jeans and pops the button off as he pulls at the waist, his fervor turns me on just that much more. He slips a finger under my soaking wet panties and in between my soft folds, and I grind against his hand.

"Mm." He moans into my breast. "Lie down on your back and let me get these jeans all the way off you."

"Yes, my Alpha."

He pauses in his dexterous probing and looks up into my eyes, crystal blue irises flashing. "I'm not sure if I should feel mocked."

I laugh low in my throat and kiss the tip of his nose as I pull away from his hand to obey the sexy beast in my bed. "Never, my Alpha."

His dick throbs when I say it again. "Okay, never mind. That is so fucking hot. You can call me your Alpha all you fucking want." He rolls over on top of me and starts to finger-fuck me again while his tongue slides into my mouth.

My moans turn to screams as his hand pistons into me, and though I try to hold back, I find myself bucking against him. He rubs his thumb against my clit as his calloused fingers work my pussy, sparking fresh fire in my groin, and within seconds I'm coming hard. My back arches, pushing my breasts against his chest, and my voice breaks with my screaming.

Once I've been satisfied, Holden grabs my jeans again and rips them clean in half. He pulls the ruined pants off my legs and does the same to my lacy underwear.

"Hey! Those were expensive!"

He growls and positions himself between my spread-eagled legs. "Waste of fucking fabric if you ask me." Holden's breath heats my sex and his lips brush against mine when he says it, and I shudder. His mouth dives onto my pussy, and my God! I've never been devoured like this. I thread my fingers into his long, silky blonde hair and grind against his face as he uses lips, tongue, teeth, and fingers to bring me to orgasm yet again.

My screams echo in the large guest room, and if he hadn't reassured me earlier about the soundproofing, I'd feel bad for the other brothers in the household. I hadn't intended this when I asked Holden to be the one to bring my lunch, but once we were in bed together, I couldn't deny myself any longer.

Holden raises up and grabs the closest piece of discarded clothing to wipe my juices from his face. He grins, flashing his teeth and dimples, and crawls forward until his hips press into mine.

His mouth tastes of my sweet cum when he bends down to kiss me again. I lick his tongue and slip my hand between us to stroke his cock again. Holden takes my hand away, though, and his tattooed arms hold mine over my head.

I whine with need. "Please," I say, eager to have him inside me.

His eyes meet mine, and the smoldering intensity in them drives me crazy. "Don't beg. You're an Alpha in your own right, Cherry. You don't ever have to beg for it." The tip of his cock teases my folds, rubs against my clit, and though all I want to do is throw my head back and close my eyes and ride him like there's no tomorrow, I maintain eye contact as he teases me. "There you go. Challenge me, Cherry. Challenge the wolf."

I keep gazing into his eyes as I bite down on his lower lip. I don't break the skin, not quite, but from the way he shudders I did something right. "Fuck me, Holden. Fuck me hard."

He slides inside me in one smooth push, and our hips pump together. We crash into each other over and over again, each time bringing me closer and closer to the edge. Holden fills me in a way that no other man ever has, and his dick rubs my pussy in deep, dark places that I didn't even know existed.

When my grunts and moans turn to screams again, he zeroes in on the spot he hit and slams into it, targeting my G-spot with his powerful thrusts. I wrap my legs around his waist and lock my ankles at the small of his back, pushing him even deeper.

Then, without warning, Holden does something new that sends my hormones into overdrive.

He breaks eye contact to nuzzle my throat. With the wolf so close, I feel like I should be worried, but instead I lean my head back to expose it more for him. His teeth clamp down over my scar, biting but not breaking the skin. It's an act of possession, of claiming, and despite how much it turns me on, I know I'll have to discuss it with him after.

Nobody owns me. Not anymore, not ever again.

Holden bites and sucks my neck as he pounds into

me, and within minutes I'm coming for the third time in a row. He growls against my skin as he empties his hot load inside me with short, quick thrusts.

When we're both sated, he pulls out and wraps his arms around me, rolling us to the side. We lie together like that for a long while, taking the time to catch our breath and just bask in each other's glow. I snuggle against his broad, toned chest and trace his abs with a fingertip. Holden works my hair loose from its braid and runs his hands through my silky waves.

After I've regained my senses, I decide to bring up the biting. Better now than to put it off. "Holden? Can I talk to you about something?"

His hands freeze in my hair, and I feel his shoulders slump. "Fuck. You didn't like the neck thing, did you?"

"Well…"

"Shit. I'm sorry."

I give him a playful smack in the chest. "Let me finish. My body enjoyed it very much. *Very* much. But my mind — It felt like you were trying to claim me as yours. I've said it before, Holden: no claiming ownership. I am a person, not a thing."

His hands clench into fists around my hair. "I didn't mean to. It was a heat of the moment thing. The wolf had control." He sighs and lets go of my locks to wrap his arms tighter around me for a bear hug. "Who the fuck am I kidding? The wolf lost control. *I* lost control. I should never have done that." He kisses the top of my head and rests his chin against the spot.

"No," I say with a sigh, "but I shouldn't have called you 'my Alpha,' either. That was kind of dumb, given that I won't let you claim me."

"Well, you may never be mine the way the wolf wants you to be, but I'm yours, Cherry. Even if you move on, pick one of my brothers or even another human, whatever. I don't think my wolf will ever be happy with anyone else."

"Have you ever been with another shifter — someone like you and your wolf?"

He shifts his weight and rests a hand on my hip. "Once. A friend of the family who came to my parents' funeral. Turned out, she just wanted to worm her way into an Alpha's bed to try and become a, uh, a pack mother of sorts. She tried to manipulate me into getting her pregnant, tried to trap me into a relationship so she could become the Alpha female and boss people around."

"So, not a good experience, huh?"

"The sex was okay, but yeah, I got burned. I wouldn't accept her as my official mate, and she stormed out in a huff one night. Haven't heard from her since."

"I can't imagine storming out of this place."

Holden laughs and pinches my ass. "Cherry, you were in the process of packing up to storm out of here when I brought you lunch a couple hours ago."

Oh, shit. I'd forgotten all about that. "Well, in my defense, your brother called me a tease. My feelings were hurt."

"Don't leave us just yet, Cherry. Hurt feelings or no, you should stay here until the whole murder-slash-arson thing blows over. Stay until Geiger and I can check out the biker gang more closely, and Rick and Billy will make sure Eric's brother doesn't ever bother you. We'll take care of you as long as we can. You have my word."

I inhale deep through my nose then sigh. Even to my human senses, Holden and I reek of sweat and sex. I need another shower.

"Fuck."

"Is that a command or a curse?"

I smack his shoulder as I sit up. "A curse. We both need a shower, which means I have to take a walk of shame down the hall."

Holden props himself up on an elbow. "You do realize they'll still smell me on you for a while, even after you shower." He sucks in a breath and reaches for my neck. "Then there's this beast. Fuck, I *really* lost control there."

My scar is tender when he brushes his fingers over it. I reach for the nightstand, where I've got a makeup bag with a compact mirror in it. I open the compact and inspect the damage. A reddish-purple mark the size of my palm is already visible on top of my scar, with two curved rows of little red indents from Holden's teeth, and within the mark my scar has turned back to the same bright, angry red it had before Holden healed me. "Oh, shit. That's the biggest fucking hickey I've ever had."

Holden grabs my hips and pulls me back until my ass presses against his hard-on. "Okay, I know my brothers are going to hate that, but to me, that is the sexiest fucking thing I've ever seen."

"Hey! No more of that right now." I swat at his hands and stand up, scanning the room for the discarded bathrobe from this morning. I finally find it shoved into my carry-on bag. I guess Hysterical Me thought I'd take it with me as a souvenir when I made

my dramatic exit. "We both need to take a shower—
separate showers!—before either of us goes back to face
the music."

He stretches and yawns, rolling onto his back so his
huge, tattooed dick stands straight out from his pelvis.
"'Face the music'? As the Alpha, I have no music to
face. Oh, sure, they'll all be pissed, but none of them is
going to start shit with me over this."

"Jerk!" I toss a blanket over his hips to cover his
temptation. "Stupid Alpha male attitude."

"C'mon, I didn't mean it like that."

I stick out my tongue and flick him off with a grin
as I open the door to head to the shower. I'm grateful
that I make it from the guest room to the bathroom
without running into any of the brothers. No one
knocks on the bathroom door while I'm in there, and
just when I think I'm going to make it back to my room
scot free, I open the door to find Matt sulking in the
hallway outside.

Chapter 9

He's leaning against the wall outside the bathroom with his arms crossed over his chest, his shoulders slumped, and a sour look on his face.

Shit. Face the music time. "Hey, Matt."

When he raises his eyes to meet my gaze, the crystalline blue of the wolf is present. He inhales deep, his nostrils flaring, and when he exhales it's in a frustrated sigh. "So. Made your choice then. That was quick." He looks away with a slight sneer to his lips.

"That's not fair, Matt."

"No, it's fucking not." He pushes off from the wall and moves to leave, but I grab his arm to stop him.

"Matt, would you stop for a minute? No 'choice' has been made, for fuck's sake."

He whips around and pries my hand off his arm. His grip hurts my wrist, but I fight to school my expression so he doesn't see that he's hurting me. "Funny way to phrase it, because it smells like fuck's sake is the exact reason you asked Holden to bring you your fucking lunch."

Matt's face doesn't budge when my fist connects with his jaw. He grabs my fist with his other hand and holds my arms above my head. Even though he's the smallest of the wolves, there's no way I'm breaking free. I struggle anyway, because I'm pissed, and he presses me against the wall. His whole body is hard against mine, and his breathing comes quick and shallow.

"Tell your wolf," I say through gritted teeth, "that I am not a possession. I'm a person, and I'll do what I want with whom I want regardless of who your inner animal thinks I belong to."

The inner animal answers with a hard kiss, a sharp contrast to the peck he gave me last night. His tongue presses between my lips and probes my mouth, and I find myself probing back despite my anger. My nipples harden against his muscular chest, and one of my legs raises to his hip of its own accord.

With a savage, primal growl he lets go of one arm to lift my other leg so I'm gripping his hips with my thighs. I use my free hand to take hold of his hair and turn the kiss even more aggressive as his hips pump into mine. His hard cock rubs me through our layers of clothes.

This isn't how I want it to be with Matt. Matt makes me think of safety and sweetness, not this harsh, angry humping. I've gotta stop this before we end up doing something we both regret.

I break free from the kiss and pull his head back by the hair, exposing his neck. Drawing on the confidence given by Holden's claims of my dominance, I place my mouth over Matt's jugular and bite down. I growl and squeeze my jaws, but I'm careful not to break the skin. I don't want to hurt him, just to get him — and his wolf — to calm down.

Matt freezes mid-hump and whines. He lets go of my arm and leg to support my lower back with his arms.

I keep my teeth on his throat until I'm standing again with both feet on the floor. Once I'm sure that he's not going to get aggressive again, I let go and meet his eyes, which are transitioning back to the darker, human shade. Tears fill those eyes, and I wonder if they're tears of hurt, of rage, or of something else.

"That wasn't the same Matt from last night."

He averts his eyes and lets me go. "You're a quick study."

I point at my own neck. "I had a long, hard lesson."

He barks out a dry chuckle. "Long and hard, all right."

This time he has the decency to let his head whip around when I give him the smack to the face he deserves. "What the hell is wrong with you?"

"I don't know." Matt's voice is soft, so soft it breaks on the last word. The tears spill from his eyes, and his gorgeous face crumples. "You just—you are so hot, and half the time you smell turned on. And we had a nice little talk last night, so I had hoped … but that was stupid of me. You're a strong woman; of course you and Holden would be a match."

I throw my hands up in the air and take a few steps back before I end up hitting Matt a third time. "What is with you guys and trying to assign ownership of me?"

Matt winces as though I had hit him again. "I'm sorry. I know you don't like that."

"Look, maybe I should have Holden call another household meeting, or whatever you guys call it. I need to lay down some ground rules. With *all* of you."

"Please, Cherry, don't get Holden involved. If he finds out I almost—" He gulps, and his eyes jerk back and forth as he scans the hallway, I assume to see if Holden's nearby. He drops his voice to a whisper again. "Cherry, I almost raped you just now. If you hadn't taken control, I don't think I could have stopped myself."

Oh, geez. This poor guy. I step closer and reach out to touch his face where I smacked him. I stroke the smooth skin of his jaw with my thumb. "Matt, you didn't 'almost rape' me. We came close to having very angry sex, but I stopped you not because I don't want to have sex with you, but because I didn't want to have that kind of sex with you. Sweet sex, tender sex, sure, but I don't want to have angry sex with you. I don't want to be angry with you, and I don't want you angry with me."

Matt closes his eyes and leans into my touch. "You'd have sex with me? Even after you've been with Holden?"

"Well," I chuckle low in my throat and kiss his cheek, "maybe not this *soon* after I've been with someone else. But yes. I'd still have sex with you, Matt. You're a hot guy in your own right; you shouldn't discount yourself just because you're not the Alpha."

His arms wrap around me in a gentle hug, and I hug back. We stand like that for a few moments while he finishes his cry. "Sweet and tender?" he says through the last of the sniffles.

"With you? Absolutely."

Matt nods and pulls back. "Okay. Let's make a date for it."

"Ooh, a proper date, huh?" That's adorable.

"Well, I happen to know that Holden and Geiger are going into town tomorrow to check out that biker gang you mentioned, and Rick and Billy are going to go rough up — well, scare at least — that brother of Eric's." He grins and winks. "I drew guard duty here with you, so we'll be alone most of the day."

I can't help but smile. His enthusiasm for our date is just too cute. "Lunch and a movie, maybe? Do you guys have a DVD player or streaming service or something here?"

Matt perks up, and I imagine that if he was in wolf form his ears would be cocked forward and his tail would be in full wag. "We've got tons of movies. What would you like to watch?"

"Surprise me."

I leave Matt in the hallway with a smile and a wave and a blown kiss goodbye, and I go back to my room.

Chapter 10

Holden's gone when I get back to the guest room, so I assume he went to shower and take care of Alpha stuff. I don't know quite what that entails, but I suppose if it was any of my business he'd tell me about it.

I grab my laptop from where I'd set it on the dresser and sit down on the bed — which I notice has fresh, clean sheets on it — to do some research. I've still got my mind set on creating some ground rules between myself and the pack, but I need to know more about wolf behavior before I do that.

I also need their wi-fi password. Fuck.

I don't know where Holden is, and Matt has most likely run off somewhere to start setting up for our date tomorrow. Rick and Billy, I suspect, are still angry with me, so I decide to search for Geiger.

I find him in the great room a few minutes later, reading a book. "Hey, Geiger? What's your wi-fi password?"

He rattles off a string of numbers and letters, and I struggle to type them in one-handed while I balance the laptop on my other arm. After a few attempts, I'm in. I smile and give him a cheerful "Thanks" before heading back down the hall.

Back at my room, I shut the door behind me and type "wolf behavior" into the search engine. The first result is a nonprofit wolf preservation charity's website, so I figure that's as good a place to start as any.

I find the usual stuff about dominance and submission, behavior, territory, *et cetera*. Then I come to the section about mating and reproduction.

This site says that most wolves mate for life.

Shit.

That isn't what I'd hoped to read. Not with the problems I've had since I got here.

I do some more digging, and depending on which site I go to, I get different answers. Most suggest that the dominant pair — that would be Holden and me — tend to stick together when it comes to mating, unless something happens to one of them, in which case another wolf in the pack can take the place of the missing mate. I don't want anything to happen to Holden, but all this mating business is confusing enough without having my decision, if I even want to make one yet, made for me.

Eric thought he was the alpha type. He thought he *owned* me, that just because he took my virginity he had sole claim on me for the rest of my life. I don't even know if Eric would have held onto me that long, unless out of sheer stubborn pride, but I do know he thought that claim gave him exclusive rights that I never agreed to.

I don't think Holden's like that, and I hope I can convince the others to give me a chance to figure things out for myself, but I fear the wolves inside the men I'm living with might all have that life-bond mentality.

After breaking things off with Eric, I went a little overboard. I had been suppressed so much by his possessiveness that I got a little wild with my sexuality, often taking home bar patrons that I'd only just met.

One-night stands were refreshing after the stifling relationship with Eric, and I enjoyed experiencing a variety of partners.

A few times, just for shits and giggles, I brought home a couple of guys at once. That was fun.

Not that I'm sure I want to try that with any of the brothers. That might be a tad *too* kinky.

A knock on the door brings me back to myself, and I glance up from the screen. "Come in."

Geiger pushes the door open and leans against the frame. My eyes sweep up and down his body of their own accord, taking in his tight jeans and bulging muscles, and I curse myself for my lack of self-control when it comes to these unnaturally hot men.

"Hey. What's up?"

He takes a few steps into the room and hooks his thumbs in his pockets. "Dinner's in a few minutes. We wanted to see if you'd like to eat with us."

"What's on the menu?" I don't know why I ask. I'm starving. They could be serving raw moose carcass, and I'd still dig in.

Do moose even live in this area? Hm.

"Steak and potatoes. Probably a side salad."

"Yeah, sure. That sounds delicious, actually." I move to close the laptop, but Geiger's faster. He takes the device from me with a gentle hand, and I swallow hard as he runs his finger over the trackpad and clicks a few things. One corner of his generous mouth twitches up as he looks at my screen.

"You know," he says as he hands it back to me, "we're only part wolf. This might help you a little bit, but keep in mind that we're all human as well, and humans have their own complex series of mating behaviors."

A flush heats my cheeks as I take the laptop and see my search history open on the screen. "Geiger, I—"

He shakes his head and ruffles my hair. "No need to explain. You're curious; I get it. I'm just glad you didn't type in 'werewolf mating behavior.' Searches like that are likely to get you more myth than anything, and they might even take you to some rather unscrupulous sites."

I giggle at the thought of coming across a slew of werewolf porn sites. "Thanks for the advice."

"Find anything useful?"

With a heavy sigh, I shut the laptop and stand up to follow Geiger for dinner. "Not really. A lot of contradicting answers to a rather pressing question."

"You want to know if we mate for life."

There's that blush again. Damnit. "I want to know if I'm going to be forced to make a choice that I'm not even sure I want to make."

Geiger puts the arm with the Maori sleeve around my shoulder, and we start walking towards the great room. "No one here is going to force you—*ever*. You take all the time you need. Whatever you do or don't choose is up to you. Just a fair warning: each of us has hopes when it comes to you, and hopes crushed are dangerous for the wolves. We're very keyed into our emotions. The tension is only going to get worse the longer you're here. Oh, we'll survive it; we're not going to kill each other over it or anything. But things will get tense."

"What does your wolf hope for?" I might regret asking, but we're still alone, so…

"My wolf hopes for a chance to be with you."

"Forever?"

He squeezes my shoulder. "For as long as you'll have me."

The great room is empty when we get there, and Geiger guides me through to the dining room. A huge mahogany table sits in the center, with eight matching chairs around it, six of them with places set, and an oak china cabinet sits in the back corner. A tasteful photo collage takes up one wall, and I walk out from under Geiger's arm to check out the pictures.

From the looks of it, they're family photos. There's a young, attractive couple at their wedding — the brothers' parents, I assume — along with photos of the couple at various stages of parenthood, complete with a bath time photo of the five boys as toddlers that I can't help but giggle at.

Their mother was gorgeous. I see where they get their sandy-colored hair, but their eyes, as well as their physiques, come from their father. Their mom had clear green eyes, similar to my own, and her frame, though large and muscular by human standards, was much smaller than the male wolves' bodies.

A framed wedding invitation sits near the center of the collage, and I read off the names: Melody Mariah Gelle and William Marcus Hunter.

So, the brothers' last name is Hunter.

Strong arms wrap around me from behind, and I look down to see Holden's smoking skulls. "Dinner's almost ready."

"M'kay. Which place is mine?"

He releases me and steps back. "Here. Sit at this end. I always sit at the head of the table, and I made sure Matt set the places so you'd have some space between you and the rest of us. That way, no one gets riled up because you're sitting right next to someone that's not them."

"Thanks." I reach for the heavy wooden chair, but Holden pulls it back from the table for me and pushes it in once I'm seated.

Holden takes his place at the other end, and the brothers file in. Geiger takes a seat in the middle of one side, with one space between him and me, and Rick and Billy tussle a bit before Rick eventually wins the chair across from Geiger. Matt carries a huge tray loaded with plates of food. He dispenses dinner to everyone before taking his own seat between Geiger and Holden.

I'm not sure what everyone's waiting for, but no one picks up any silverware, and it's not long before five pairs of ocean blue eyes are staring at me. "Do you guys say Grace first or something?"

Holden's dimples pop as he grins. "We're waiting for our guest to start eating before we dig in."

"Oh! Shit." I grab my fork and knife and cut a piece from my steak. The guys all watch, which makes for some awkward screeching and scraping of the silverware on the plate. Once I've taken a bite, chewed it, and swallowed, they all sit back and start on their own meals.

"So, anyone have any news tonight?" Holden talks like he's holding another meeting. I'm not sure if this is his version of "How was everyone's day today," but it sounds weird.

Geiger finishes his bite and sets down his silverware. He dabs the corner of his mouth before he speaks. "I've got an address for the biker gang's main clubhouse. I figure you and I could go check it out tomorrow morning, when there's likely less activity. Oh, and Rick, Billy, I also found Eric's brother's address. Bishop lives on the far side of town, and from what I was able to find online he has no job, so he should be at home when you get there."

"Remember," Holden says, "you two are just going to talk to him. Scare him at most. Don't start a fight with the guy. We don't need any more potential legal trouble on our plates."

Rick ducks his head and looks away. "We know. Rile him up, not rough him up."

"Unless the dick starts something himself," Billy adds, but a glare from Holden shuts him right up.

I think back on my conversation with Holden earlier. He said that I need to confront the brother who called me a tease on my own. I could approach Rick and Billy when they're alone, but I've got a captive audience right now. "So, was it Rick or Billy who called me a 'fucking tease' this afternoon?"

All five guys freeze mid-chew, and Billy's eyes go wide. He swallows hard, his Adam's apple bobbing, and clears his throat. "I, uh, didn't know you heard that."

"Well, I did hear it. Loud and fucking clear."

His face blanches, then blooms bright red as he flushes. "I didn't mean—"

"Oh, you meant it. When, exactly, did I tease you?" I set my elbows on the table, ignoring manners in favor of dramatic effect, and rest my chin in my hands. "Go ahead, tell me when it was. Tell me the exact moment I teased you."

"Well, there wasn't an *exact* moment ..." He trails

off, eyes glued to his plate.

"Okay. What's the vague moment I teased you?"

"I..."

I lean forward and put a hand to my ear. "Hmm?"

He clamps his mouth shut, and I think I see tears brimming in his eyes.

"Okay, then. So I *didn't* tease you at any point."

Rick snickers.

"You can kindly shut the fuck up as well, Rick. I've been over this with some of you, but I guess it's necessary for me to state the obvious for the whole pack. I. Am. Not. Property. I don't belong to any one person, and I will do what I want with whom I want. If that means having lunch in my room with Holden or going to the woods with Rick and Billy to visit my grandma's grave, or whatever else strikes my fancy, that's what I'm going to do." I meet each pair of eyes, one by one, and I maintain my gaze until they look away first. Even Holden averts his eyes, though I suspect he does it on purpose to show deference to me in this matter. "Anyone else have any notions of teasing or any other such ridiculous claims about me?"

A resounding "no, ma'am" greets me from five chastised mouths.

"Good. Now let's finish this fucking awkward meal and watch a movie or something. I've had an emotional twenty-four hours, and I could use some entertainment."

Chapter 11

We finish our food in relative silence, and I'm the first to get up to take my dishes to the kitchen. Matt hops out of his chair to offer to help me, but I wave him off and take my own shit. He follows me anyway, and once we've both put our dishes in the sink and rinsed them off, he throws his arms around my neck for a quick hug.

"I'm sorry."

I sigh and step out of his arms. "We've been over this. You don't need to apologize again."

His soulful blue eyes bore into me. "It bears repeating."

I dismiss it with a wave of my hand. "After dinner tonight, I'm considering all apologies rendered and accepted in full. Clean slates all around. Now, what do you have that's animated, PG-rated, and will have me laughing so hard I pee my pants?"

We gather in the great room a few minutes later, after Matt pops several bags of popcorn, and he grabs the remote and searches the menu on their smart TV. He settles on a cartoon about talking pets, and for the next hour and forty-three minutes, I laugh my butt off, I giggle like a little kid, and in the end, I cry happy tears. I don't laugh so hard I pee my pants, but all in all it was a good choice.

Once the credits roll, I stand up and stretch, working the kinks out of my back. "Okay. Time for this little lady to go to bed." I wait for offers to help me into bed or snide comments, but none come. Good. That means they were listening at dinner. I turn to Holden. "What time do you guys start getting up in the morning?"

"Anywhere from five or six to about ten. Depends on which of us you're talking about."

That gives me pause. I want to do something in the morning, but I need all the brothers up and at 'em for it. "Everyone should be up by seven thirty tomorrow. Set some alarms if you have to. I'll see you in the dining room."

Holden raises a brow but doesn't object. "You heard the lady, guys. Seven thirty. Don't be late for — whatever she's got up her sleeve."

There's some grumbling from Rick and Billy, but Matt grins, and Geiger nods.

Once back in my room, I set my own alarm on my phone, typing in six thirty a.m. for my wake-up time. Someone cleaned the phone off for me after my bloody attempt at calling for help when Eric sliced me, but there's still some dried blood in the nooks and crannies. I spend about ten minutes with some Q-tips and rubbing alcohol before declaring it a lost cause. I'm going to need a new phone soon. I can't keep using this one, not with the blood as a constant reminder of last night.

Was it really only last night? Strange how much life can change in a day.

After going down the hall to brush my teeth and wash my face, I change into some flannel pajamas and snuggle under the plush covers of the bed. Within minutes, I'm asleep.

*   *   *

My alarm jerks me awake in the morning, and I groan as sunlight assaults me through the sheer curtains of the guest room. I lie there for a minute, hating mornings and sunlight and my own stupid ass for wanting to do something nice for the brothers, then I haul myself up out of bed with a sigh and head for the bathroom. I've got a little bit of time to shower and get dressed before the brothers start filing in—I hope.

I opt for simple today, with a green tank top and some khaki-colored yoga pants. My hair goes up in a wavy ponytail, and I throw on some cute socks with cherries on them. What can I say? I own a lot of cherry-themed clothing.

I don't know Holden's policy on shoes inside the house—frankly, I haven't paid attention to whether or not the brothers have been wearing them inside—but I figure some simple flats won't harm the floors.

I don't run into any of the Hunter brothers on my way to the kitchen, which I find surprising. If some of them get up around five or six on a normal day, where are they?

It doesn't take much digging in the fridge to find what I need. Eggs, sausage, bacon, mushrooms, onions, tomatoes, peppers, cheese, salt, pepper, garlic—they've got everything I need to make them some bomb omelets, and in werewolf-sized quantities at that.

The dishes and pans clatter so much I fear that none of them will need alarms for breakfast, but no one comes to see what I'm up to.

At least, no one comes in until about seven fifteen, when a groggy, half-naked Matt enters the kitchen and wordlessly starts grabbing cups and silverware to set the table.

"Morning, Matt!" I chirp as I pour the raw eggs into the five frying pans I've set out on the massive stove. Their kitchen, which I hadn't taken the time to appreciate earlier, has an amazing setup for cooking large amounts of food. I've already gotten two cups of coffee in me, so I don't take offense when Matt simply groans in response.

He must be one of the ones who usually gets up closer to ten.

"You're a sadist, you know," he says when he gets back from setting the table. "Need any help?"

"Nope." I sprinkle the chopped veggies on the eggs. "I got this."

Matt groans again and rubs his eyes. He fumbles in the cabinet for a coffee mug and fills it from the pot I made. "Seven fucking thirty."

I stick my tongue out and wave the spatula at him. "Not my fault you decided to get up early to set the table. I was going to get that, you know."

"Mm. Well, I beat you to it." He grabs an extra spatula to start helping with the omelets, but I snatch it from his hand.

"Hey! This is my treat to you guys for all your help. You don't get to help with my token of appreciation for your help; I'll be in an endless cycle of debt if you do that." I do my best admonishing glare, but he just grins and kisses my nose.

"You're adorable when you're asserting yourself, you know," he says, his lips tickling my nose.

"Hush. You know you love it. Now go sit down at the table. Breakfast will be ready soon."

Matt salutes me as he backs into the dining room.

Ten minutes later, I manage to carry the heavy tray of omelets into the dining room without dropping anything, and to my delight all five Hunter brothers sit gathered around the table. Holden and Geiger are already dressed for the day in tight polo shirts and khakis, but, like Matt, Rick and Billy are still in pajama bottoms.

"Morning, Hunters!"

My cheery greeting is met with mixed reactions. Holden and Geiger grin and Matt smiles from ear to ear and jumps up to help distribute the plates, but Rick and Billy's eyes are half lidded. I wonder if they'll be able to stay awake long enough to eat their food.

"How'd everyone sleep last night?"

Billy props his head up on one hand and pokes at his omelet with a fork. "Are we being punished again?"

I stop on my way to put the tray back in the kitchen. "Huh?"

He points at my empty place setting. "We've all gotta get up early for this, but you're not even eating. What is this about?"

"Oh, that. I don't usually eat much for breakfast. I snacked on some of the veggies while I was cooking these up. I just thought I'd treat all of you to a nice meal before you went off on your missions today."

"We had to get up early for that? Why not just make it when we're all up?"

I roll my eyes. "It won't kill you to be up and ready early, and I wasn't about to cook five separate meals at different times."

"You couldn't find a happier medium?" Rick grumbles.

"Seven thirty is halfway between five and ten.

That's the medium. Now shut up and eat."

Rick takes a bite, and in an instant his eyebrows shoot up. He stares at me with awe in his eyes, then shoots a glare at Holden. "How come we never get breakfast that's this good? You've been holding out on us!"

Holden and Geiger exchange a glance while Matt snickers. "If you'd get up before ten, you might get some decent food too."

"Or cook it yourself," Geiger offers between bites. "I, for one, was up at five, and she didn't exactly sneak out to go to the store. She found all this—" he waves at the plates of food "—here in our very own kitchen."

Billy throws his hands in the air mid-bite. "There's never omelets in the fucking kitchen when I go in there!"

"As Geiger said, you can cook it yourself. All the ingredients are in there." I put a hand on my hip and wave the tray in the direction of the kitchen.

"Ingredients, sure, but where's the food?"

Rick scrapes the last of the cheese and egg from his plate and shoves it in his mouth. "I, for one, appreciate this, Cherry. I really do. No one's fed us breakfast like this since … well, in a long time." He raises his glass of juice in salute. "To Cherry!"

The other four raise their glasses and clink them against Rick's. "To Cherry!"

I exit with a dramatic bow and go back to the kitchen to start cleanup.

Holden and Rick join me moments later, rinsing their empty plates in the sink before taking the dirty pans from me and taking over the washing.

"You guys don't have to do that, you know."

Holden nods and dries the pans and dishes that Rick hands him. "We know. We just finished first, so we got dibs on helping. You don't have to do any of this, either. You're our guest, and you're making us look bad." His tone is serious, but his dimples pop, giving him away.

I pour myself a third cup of coffee as Matt and Billy join in the cleanup efforts by starting on the stove and countertops. Geiger finishes his breakfast last, and with no tasks left to do, he leans against the counter next to me and sips on the last of the coffee. As I start to get the coffee maker ready for another pot, because I'm sure some of the boys will want more, Geiger stops me and does it himself.

"I've got to hand it to you," he says as he scoops the grounds into the filter, "I don't think anyone except Mom has ever been able to get all five of us to clean anything together."

"Hey, don't look at me. You all volunteered. I didn't do anything here."

"Well, whatever you're not doing, keep it up. We could use some cohesion around here." He smiles as he pushes buttons on the coffee maker and gets another pot started.

I snort into my mug and give Geiger a wry grin. "I seem to be more of a divisive influence than cohesive."

"All depends on how you look at it," Holden says as he tosses the towel over his shoulder and puts away the last of the dishes. "I mean, we're all in agreement about certain aspects of you spending time here—just not necessarily in agreement about who should be allowed to enjoy that time with you."

I roll my eyes at his choice of phrase and set my

empty mug on the counter with a *clink*. "And on that note, I'm going to spend some time in the great room watching TV. You guys have WebFlicks, right?"

Holden nods.

"Cool. There's a show I've been dying to see, but I can't afford a subscription right now." I push off from the counter and head for the great room. "Anyone who wants to join me before they go out for the day is welcome. It's a sci-fi series called *Orion's Calling*. We could maybe binge a couple episodes before everyone heads out?" I look back to see if anyone's taking the bait.

Geiger shakes his head. "Holden and I have to start early today. Maybe Matt, Billy, and Rick could watch some with you before Billy and Rick have to leave, though."

I shrug and go in search of the remote. Once I've found it, I plop down on the middle seat of the couch and start flipping through the TV apps until I find WebFlicks. *Orion's Calling* is one of their more popular shows, but it takes me a bit of searching to find it. I guess the Hunter brothers aren't much for sci-fi, because their most-watched shows include a bunch of bloody explosion action flicks. Typical.

Rick, Billy, and Matt file in just as the credits start, and though Matt's at the head of the line, he chooses to sit on the floor at my feet rather than on the couch next to me. It's a smart choice, I guess, because from what I've seen so far Rick and Billy seem to prefer the couch as their territory, and it also lets all three men sit next to me without anyone being left out.

I also suspect that Matt, knowing full well that he'll have me all to himself in a little while, doesn't care about his brothers being next to me on the couch for the time being.

Holden and Geiger wave goodbye as they head out the front door, and it's just me and the other three.

The show starts slow, but as the episode gets further in the plot becomes more evident, and by the end of the second episode I'm hooked. I'll have to hang out here at least long enough to catch up on the whole season—if I go home too soon, I'll never know what happens to Captain Hardigan and his crew.

Rick and Billy excuse themselves to go confront Eric's brother, and now Matt has me all to himself. He looks up at me with a wolfish grin, and a lock of sandy hair flops into his eyes. I brush it away and smile back. "So, is this a good time to start our date?"

He nods and stands, pulling me up with him. "Go on; get ready. I gotta get the room set up."

I look down at what I'm wearing. "You don't like this?"

Matt cocks his head to the side and frowns at me. "Why do you say that?"

"You just told me to get ready. I thought this outfit was kinda cute." I don't mention the cherry-printed thong I have on under the yoga pants. That's for later.

"It is. I just thought girls did stuff before a date."

This makes me laugh. "What kind of 'stuff' did you think us girls do?"

He shrugs. "Makeup. Perfume. Stuff."

I give him a playful shove and laugh again. "Holden told me you guys don't like strong smells like perfume, so I've been avoiding it here. And are you saying I need makeup? Is my natural face not good enough?"

I think Matt takes me seriously, because he turns red and gulps. "No! You're gorgeous. I just thought—"

"I'm teasing, Matt. If you want to do something special with the great room, then I'll go to my room for however long you need to do that, but as far as I'm concerned, at least, I'm ready for our date already."

He places his hands on my shoulders and pushes me towards the hallway. "Give me ten—no, fifteen minutes. I'll come get you when I'm done."

Chapter 12

I grin as I walk back to my room and sit on the bed. Ten or fifteen minutes isn't much, but I get bored with waiting before too long and pull out my phone to check my texts and social media.

My grin disappears as I see multiple texts from Bishop with gruesome, detailed threats of rape and murder, and a few of the biker gang members have taken to WebPlace to call me out and threaten me as well. None of them seem to know where I am, but there are plenty of assurances that they'll find me and do unspeakable things to me — well, unspeakable for me, but they have no qualms about voicing them. Some of the things they describe bring a surge of bile to the back of my throat, and I have to stamp it down before I end up running to the bathroom to puke. These guys are sick.

A soft knock on the door makes me jump, until I remember Matt. "Come in."

He opens the door a crack and pokes his head in. "Ready?"

I heave a sigh and hold the phone out to him. "Mind forwarding some shit to Holden and your brothers for me? I don't have any of their numbers, but they're going to want to see this."

Matt takes the phone, flips through the screenshots I took, and curses. "Those fuckers!"

"Yeah. Makes me glad I don't have to go home any

time soon."

"Fuck. So much for our date."

I frown at him. "Huh? Why can't we still have our date? It's not like we're going anywhere. These guys don't know I'm here, and yeah, it's a downer, but I'm not going to let it stop us. Just forward those screenshots to Holden and everyone, and then we'll go watch the movie you picked out."

He pulls his own phone out of his pocket after playing with mine for a bit, I assume sending himself the screenshots so it's easier to forward them. I notice that his eyes are shifting to crystal blue. "My wolf is not happy about this, and my brothers' wolves won't be, either. They're going to want blood. Rick and Billy might just kill that Bishop asshole when they see this, and I hate to think what kind of mess Holden and Geiger will get into with the gang. Westside Mayhem? Fucking cuntwaffles is what their name should be."

I wait for him to finish with his phone, then get up and put my hands on his shoulders. "Tell the wolf to calm down. I'm safe here, safe with you, and right now is our time. You and me, Matt; you promised me a proper date today."

Matt's phone buzzes in his hand, and I take it from him. "Hey, Holden."

"What the hell is this that Matt's sending us? Are these all from your phone?"

"Yeah. Bishop and the gang are out for blood, looks like. I thought you'd want to see those before you got too far into whatever you're doing today."

"Let me talk to Matt."

I hand him the phone. He wraps his other arm around me and pulls me close. "Yeah. No, trust me, I'm not letting her out of my sight. Yeah. Yeah, okay. Just keep in touch if you need me to send Rick and Billy over your way. Okay, bro. Bye." He hangs up and completes the hug. "You, Miss Cherry, now have a shadow. I'm not to let you out of my sight for anything—and Holden did emphasize *anything*—today or any other time I'm on guard duty."

"Guard duty doesn't sound very romantic." I give him a little pout.

"Oh, we'll still have our date. Makes it easier to watch you." He winks. "Now c'mon, let's go back to the other room. I came in here to tell you it's all set up."

He takes my hand and guides me to the great room, which has been transformed. The couch and other chairs are gone, and in the middle of the floor lies a mound of pillows and blankets inside a circle of lit candles. Dark curtains line the room, except for the wall with the fireplace and the TV screen, where the curtains have been tied back with thick ropes. The whole look gives the great room the appearance of a movie theater, and I suspect the pillows and blankets will be just as soft as any others I've encountered in this house. The wolves must really like plush textures.

"Oh, Matt, it's gorgeous! How did you do all this in such a short time?"

He kisses my cheek. "I was highly motivated."

Before I have a chance to walk over to the bed of pillows, Matt sweeps me off my feet and carries me there, stepping over the candles and placing me in the lush pile. He settles in behind me, taking a place as the big spoon, and grabs the remote. "I found a good movie. It's about werewolves, but it's more of a romance than a bloody gore movie."

I raise a brow and look back at him. "It had better not be that tweeny bopper movie."

Matt snorts with laughter and kisses me. "No, my sweet Cherry, it's not that one. This one's actually a decent film."

"Good. I might have to disown the whole pack if any of you watch that crap."

"Never."

I smile and snuggle in as Matt starts the movie. He drapes an arm over my waist and traces my belly button with idle fingers while the movie plays. I prop my head up on an elbow and reach behind me with the other hand to play with his hair. It's cropped closer than his brothers', but long enough to get in his eyes on occasion — and to be fun to play with. His hair feels silky-smooth in my fingers.

As the movie gets further in, Matt's hand starts to migrate. He traces a line from my navel to the new scar on my abdomen, and I feel him stiffen behind me as he outlines the scar with his fingertips.

I twist around and kiss him. "He's gone, Matt. He's not going to hurt me anymore."

"We startled him. Us wolves. He wouldn't have cut you if we hadn't surprised him."

"Matt." I take his face in both hands and force him to look me in the eye; his wolf is at the surface again. "Eric would have cut me regardless. He already did cut me a week before that. You guys saved me. I'd be dead right now if it wasn't for the pack."

Matt growls, and I roll the rest of the way over. His hand slides over me to my lower back, and he nudges my leg with a knee. "Make me forget, Cherry. Make me forget how we failed you."

"Sweet and tender?" I ask as I slide my leg over his hip. My hands drift down his toned chest before slipping under his shirt to better appreciate his muscles.

He kisses me, soft and sweet. "With you? Always." He tugs my shirt up, exposing my breasts, and strokes my hard nipples with a gentle touch. He chuckles with his lips still against mine. "No bra, huh? Guess you were hoping to get lucky on our date."

"I was counting on it." I shift my hips closer, rubbing my crotch against the bulge in his pants, and I receive a low moan in response. "Mm. You like that?"

He growls and clutches my breasts. "I'd like it better if our fucking clothes weren't in the way."

I sit up and pull my tank top the rest of the way off. "Like this?"

"Mm. More."

I wag a finger at him. "Uh-uh-uh! Not fair if I'm the only one getting naked here."

Matt scrambles to even the odds. He gets stuck with his shirt partway off, so I reach out to help him. When I get the shirt off his face, my breasts are right there for the taking, and Matt doesn't miss a beat. He puts his mouth over one nipple and sucks and licks until my back arches into him. One of his arms snakes around to hold me to him while the other pulls at the waist of my pants. "Your turn."

I stand with a grin and hook my thumbs in the waist of the yoga pants, lowering them inch by inch, until I'm bent in half in front of him. I step out of the pants and tug off my socks; I leave the thong on for now.

With shaking hands, Matt unbuttons his jeans and

fumbles with the zipper. When his cock finally pops free, I see that he's enjoying the show so far. He stands to shimmy out of the jeans, and I drop to my knees to help him out again. I pull both the jeans and the boxers underneath all the way down.

Before he has a chance to get down on the floor with me, I take his shaft into my hands and begin to pump with slow, steady strokes.

Matt moans and grabs my ponytail.

"Remember," I say with my lips against the tip of his cock, "sweet and tender."

He locks eyes with me and nods.

I maintain eye contact as I take him into my mouth. He tastes sweeter than Holden, but I push the thought out of my mind. Now's not the time for comparisons. I stroke and suck in alternating patterns, hands down, head back, hands up, head down, all the while rolling my tongue in circles on his veined shaft. Bit by bit, I work my mouth farther and farther down, until I've got him almost all the way in.

Matt closes his eyes, and I watch as his pecs and biceps flex in response to my actions. He wants to pump those hips, to push my head into him, I can see it in the twitching muscles, but he's holding back. I suck harder. Wet, slurping sounds come from my lips, and Matt groans.

I let go with one hand to fondle his balls, and that, it seems, is almost too much. Matt pulls my head back and kneels in front of me. "Oh, God, Cherry, I could let you do that all day, but then I wouldn't be able to take care of you." He slides the crotch of my thong to the side and rubs my clit.

It's my turn to moan, and I do so with a swirl of my

hips against his probing fingers. I bury my hand in his hair and pull his head down. "Your turn, babe."

He's timid at first, almost hesitant to pull off my thong, but I spread my legs a little more to give him some encouragement. He groans as he sees my wet pussy in front of him, and I lose yet another pair of underwear to a Hunter brother as he snaps the straps of the thong in his haste to get to me.

Matt's tongue tickles my clit as he plunges two fingers into my cunt. I hold his head to me and grind my hips against his face. I lift one leg up and over his shoulder to pull him closer, and Matt sucks on my hub of nerves as his fingers sink deeper.

Every muscle trembles as Matt works his magic. He laps up my juices as I writhe and groan, and when he slips the third finger in and sucks on my clit, I come in a spray all over his face and hand. I ride the spasms of my orgasm while Matt grabs my hip with his free hand and holds me to him as he licks it all up, moaning and growling the whole time.

Dear God, I love the animal sounds these brothers make during sex.

"Get on your hands and knees." He growls the words, and his eyes glow that brilliant crystalline blue.

My arms still shake as I follow his command, and I gasp when he enters me from behind.

True to his word, Matt takes it slow, making even the submissive position sweet and tender. He pushes all the way in, grinds, then pulls almost all the way out. In, grind, out. In, grind out. The steady rhythm drives me crazy, and I cry out with each thrust and grind. My back arches, and Matt leans in close to kiss the side of my neck.

He doesn't bite like Holden did, but his sucking and licking only serve to drive me even further towards the edge of release. Matt takes one hip in his hand to help steady me and guide his own hips while the other reaches around to massage my clit with slow, thick strokes.

In, stroke, grind, out. In, stroke, grind, out.

My cries are longer now, drawn out, as he hits that sensitive spot inside just before stroking the nerves. His timing is fucking perfect.

"Cherry," he whispers in my ear with the next thrust. "I'm so fucking close right now." He bites my lobe and tugs with his teeth, and my next moan extends as he picks up speed. "So. Fucking. Close." Each word punctuated with another thrust. Another stroke. Another grind. Another step closer to climax.

"M-matt," I say, my voice strained, sounding like a mewling kitten, "I'm close, t-too. So — Ah! — So. God. Damn. Close!"

Sweet and tender go out the window when I say that, and Matt releases my hip to massage my breast as he pumps into me with more force. The sensations that come crashing into me from all three fronts — oh, shit, all *four* fronts — as he bites, squeezes, strokes, and thrusts, all bring me to the most amazing high, and my voice breaks in a long, drawn-out scream, a primal sound that rips raw from my throat.

I shudder and collapse onto my forearms, but Matt's not done. He rides me through my orgasm, through the spasming after-effects, until finally he releases his hot seed inside me.

Matt's arms wrap around me, and he pulls me to the bed of pillows with him. He's the big spoon again, and I snuggle in close. He nuzzles my neck and kisses it before lying all the way down. I glance up at the TV and see that we've missed the entire second half of the movie; the credits are almost over.

"I guess we'll have to watch it again," I say with a giggle.

He pulls one of the blankets over us. "I'll never look at this movie the same way again."

This sparks fresh giggles from me, and Matt encourages them by starting to tickle my sides. I shriek and wiggle, and I feel him start to harden against my back again when the front door bursts open, and Holden storms in carrying a bleeding Geiger.

Chapter 13

"What the hell —" Matt jumps up to help his brothers, and I pull the blanket closer around me.

"Holden, what happened?"

Holden doesn't answer either of us, which scares me more than anything. He and Matt take Geiger straight to Holden's bedroom, and I scramble to my feet, tripping on the edge of the blanket and nearly catching the damn thing on fire when I step over the candles to follow them.

They lay Geiger down on Holden's bed, and Holden starts to strip out of his bloody clothes. "Matt, Rick and Billy are on the way, but I'll need you to stay here. I'll need all three of you if we're going to save him."

"Is there anything I can do?" I stare in horror at the sheer amount of blood seeping through Geiger's clothes. From the multiple points of saturation, my guess — at this distance, anyway — is that he's been shot.

Things must have gone bad with the Westside Mayhem.

Matt and Holden turn in unison, as though my voice startled them. Holden's eyes are wolf-blue, and he's sweating. "Go to the guest room. Shut the door, lock it, and stay put. Don't let anyone in unless it's one of us."

Matt looks at his Alpha. "You think you were followed?"

Holden shakes his head. "I don't know, but if we were, I need to know Cherry's safe. I can't focus if she's not."

I put a hand on my hip and stand to my full height—not impressive, given the company, but I figure good posture can't hurt when trying to assert myself. "Cherry is in the fucking room, guys, and she doesn't appreciate being talked about like this. Now, I can help. I might not be a nurse or anything, but I can run and get bandages or hot water or something if you just tell me where and what to get. Then, once you have everything you need, I'll come back and sit in the fucking corner and stay out of your way." Holden opens his mouth, probably to argue, but I'm not stopping. "Before you say it, I'll be safer in this room with the five of you than in the guest room by myself."

He growls and shoves Matt towards me. "Take her and get some hot water going. Get towels—lots of them—and grab the fucking med kit, too. I'll need to sedate him. For now, I'll hold pressure where I can until you guys get back."

I hike the blanket up higher and follow Matt's lead.

The first stop is the hall bathroom. He tosses me one of the robes, and I put it on while Matt pulls pile after pile of thick, white towels out of the cabinet. "Carry these back and stay with Holden and Geiger. I'll get the meds and start the hot water."

"That's it? You're going to have me carry towels and nothing else? I can start the water going or something, too."

"No. It's quicker if I do it. Besides, there's a door to the outside in the kitchen, and I don't want you near any outer doors right now. Neither does Holden, I'm sure. Just go back and help Holden where you can. Please, Cherry. Be safe for us."

I don't like being relegated to Towel Girl, but seeing the fear in Matt's eyes, I bite my tongue on my retort and head back to the master bedroom.

Holden's got Geiger stripped down, and he's holding scraps of Geiger's clothes against two of the wounds. Once I get close with the towels, I can see that they are indeed bullet wounds. There's a first aid kit open on the huge bed, the contents scattered as though Holden had just dumped the thing in his search for whatever he needed.

I hand Holden the towels and step back into the corner, as promised. I'm not there long, though, because Holden waves for me to come back over.

"Here. Take this towel and hold pressure on his shoulder. Go ahead, press hard. He's already in a shit-ton of pain, he'll hardly notice it."

I do as ordered, and Geiger growls a little.

"Don't worry. He won't hurt you." He hands me another towel. "That bullet went straight through, so you'll have to press on both sides. Again, press hard. Whatever you do, don't let go, and don't shrink back when he growls. His wolf is close, and it can smell your fear when he does that. Our wolves are pissy enough when we're not vulnerable; you don't want to make it even angrier now."

"My arms are too short. I can't reach from over here."

"Well, then, climb on up and get behind his head. You should be able to reach from there, right?"

I nod and get into a kneeling position next to Geiger's head. With both hands occupied, I'm helpless to do anything but hold the pressure while Holden gets to work. The towels are soaked within seconds, and I feel the hot blood against my skin.

"He'll be okay, right? I mean, what are the odds that the Mayhem had silver bullets?"

Holden growls, and for the first time the sound scares me. "This isn't a fucking movie, Cherry. Regular bullets will kill us just fucking fine."

Moments later, Matt returns with a pot of hot water and a small container that reminds me of a diabetic's insulin pack. When he opens it, there are half a dozen pre-filled syringes lining the inside.

I suspect that's not insulin.

Matt yanks the cap off one of the needles and injects Geiger in the crook of his arm. The body beneath me relaxes, but only a fraction, as Geiger drifts into a semi-conscious state.

I don't envy Holden his job. He's got a wicked-looking pair of pliers or tongs or something, and he's digging around in a bullet wound with them. After what seems like an eternity of digging, he pulls out a malformed bullet and moves on to the next wound. Geiger growls louder each time the pliers go in and yelps when the bullets are pulled out. From my new vantage point, I count six wounds in total, including the one I'm holding.

When the last bullet is out, Holden grabs some small medical packages from the pile of supplies on the bed and opens one. Inside, I see a fine needle and some thread. Sutures.

Matt shoves a thick strap of leather between Geiger's teeth and holds it down.

"Why are you gagging him? We're in the middle of

nowhere; no one's going to hear him scream."

Matt gives me a sideways glance and secures the strap tighter. "But he might change if he decides that what Holden's doing is a threat. I'd rather not let him bite you. It wouldn't be fun for any of us, least of all Geiger when he wakes up."

Needle in hand, Holden motions for me to remove the towels so he can see how bad the gunshot is. He grimaces and sets his jaw. "Okay, Cherry, you're going to have to hold that bit of leather for us. I need Matt to roll him so I can stitch up the underside because he's stronger than you are. You might not be able to move him and hold him like I'll need."

I nod and scoot over so I'm straddling his head with my knees. I hold down tight on the ends of the strap as Geiger snarls with the movement of his shoulder.

As Holden starts to stitch around the wound, Rick and Billy scramble into the room, breathless, and gape as they see the scene before them. "Shit, Holden, what the fuck happened?"

"Good. Pack's all here. You guys hold his arms and legs, but be gentle with this side here."

Rick and Billy nod in unison and take hold of Geiger's limbs.

I've had stitches before, but suturing without a local anesthetic must be torture. Even with the sedative in his system, Geiger writhes and snarls as Holden sets to work closing the wounds. When the exit wound on his back is stitched shut, he moves to the front wound. The bleeding has slowed, but Holden doesn't seem to be taking any chances.

From my vantage point, I have a better view of

Holden himself, and I notice that some of the blood on his bare skin seems fresh, fresher than the rest. I look closer and realize that, with the position of the fresh, dark blood, it's likely from the bullet that passed through Geiger. He must have jumped in front of his Alpha when the shooting started, and the bullet that passed through him made it to Holden on the other side. Holden's working so hard to save his brother that either he hasn't noticed he got shot, too, or he's ignoring the pain and blood loss.

"Holden," I say as I hold the strap against Geiger's thrashing. "That bullet that went through Geiger — He wouldn't have happened to be standing in front of you when he got hit, would he?"

Holden grunts but doesn't answer.

Matt takes a moment to inspect the spot I'm talking about. Holden growls a warning at him, but Matt ignores him. I guess his position as Omega gives him some leeway in his behavior around the wounded Alpha. "Shit, Holden, with all the blood here I didn't even see that. We'll have to dig it out, you know. You're the Alpha, but you're not fucking Superman. That's gotta come out, and you'll need to be sewn up yourself."

"Geiger first," Holden growls. "Once he's all patched up, you can do whatever you want to me. Then we heal."

I remember what healing entails. Holden's going to have to hold Geiger tight in this dangerous, half-feral state, and use their pack's magic to mend the wounds.

"Matt, Rick, Billy, you three will stay in here — I'll need all of us for this — but stay the fuck alert. If the gang followed us here, Cherry could be in danger.

She's going to stay in here with us for safety, but I'd feel better about going into the healing trance if I know you guys are watching out for her."

The three brothers nod their affirmation, and Rick and Billy press down harder as Geiger bucks against their grip when Holden moves to a wound on his stomach. Matt sets to work bandaging the spots that have already been stitched.

I lose track of how long I've been kneeling there, holding the leather strap between Geiger's teeth. When Holden's gentle hand tugs at my arms to get me to let go, my fingers have cramped so hard I have trouble releasing the strap.

"We're done stitching him up. He shouldn't bite now."

I look up and see that Rick and Billy have removed their hands from Geiger's limbs. They're wiping blood from their hands with some of the towels, which by now are almost all ruined.

"What about you, Holden? Will we need this for you?" I point at the strap, then at the bleeding wound on his shoulder.

Holden shakes his head and sits down on the bed next to Geiger. "I'm not as bad off as Geiger is, Cherry. Plus, I'm the Alpha. Part of that is keeping the pack together when shit goes bad, and part of *that* is keeping my own shit together." He nods at Matt. "Go ahead. The bullet's still in there. I can feel it. Dig it out, but be quick about it."

I can't tear my eyes away as Matt shoves the weird pliers into Holden's wound and fishes for the bullet. He pulls it out with a sick *squelch* and grabs a fresh package of sutures. I marvel at Holden's ability to hold still for the procedure, but I guess that's the Alpha at work.

Once Holden's stitched and bandaged, he curls up next to Geiger and wraps his tattooed arms around his brother. The other wolves each sit down on the bed and put a hand on Holden. He looks up at me with crystalline eyes. "This won't be easy to watch, Cherry. Sometimes the wolf takes over during healing, especially when it's this bad. Are you sure you don't want to close yourself in your room until this is over?"

I shake my head and take Geiger's head into my lap. "I'm staying."

"In that case," he continues, "are you sure you don't want to take a quick shower? Geiger and his wolf are less possessive than some of the rest of us, but I suspect some of his agitation comes from your scent right now. If you smell less like Matt with Geiger's head in your crotch, his wolf is more likely to calm down a bit."

"Oh, shit!"

Holden grins, but it's a grim expression. "Just use my shower. Be quick. Despite your scent right now, I think you're having a calming influence on him."

I glance at the small master bath. "Are there any robes in there like these? I don't want to put this thing back on when it's soaked like this."

Holden nods at a dresser in the far corner of the room. "Just grab one of my t-shirts out of there. You'll be swimming in it, but smelling like his Alpha is better than this. Now go—get cleaned up."

I take the quickest shower I can while still getting thoroughly cleaned, and when I come back, Holden's in full wolf form. I swallow past a lump in my throat as I get back in position at Geiger's head. "Why did he shift? Is his wound worse than it looked?"

Matt shakes his head. "It helps with the healing. He's tapping into the most primal part of our pack magic. If Geiger wasn't so badly injured, we'd have him shift, too. That could kill him right now, though, so we're making him stay human. Really, the three of us should shift, too, but then you'd be more vulnerable. Even though we're vicious as wolves, against humans with guns it's sometimes better to be human as well." His jaw clenches as Geiger whines. "That, and we're bigger targets as humans. Broader, better shields."

"Shields?"

Rick looks over at me, his eyes serious for probably the first time that I've seen. "To protect you. If we stand in front of you as wolves, we won't be able to block the bullets as easily as we can now."

Fuck. I've ruined these brothers' lives with my stupidity. Now they're all dead set on protecting me, no matter what cost to themselves.

I turn my attention back to Geiger and stroke his hair with a gentle touch. He's covered with smeared blood, and I'm torn between getting some washcloths to clean him off and staying here, where my touch seems to help.

Geiger's eyes flutter open, and though the wolf is present, his voice is more human. "Cherry." He breathes my name, like just saying it sustains him as much as air. "Stay with me. Please."

If I hadn't seen what I'd seen since meeting the Hunter brothers, I might be surprised at the timing of his request. It's almost like he knew what I was thinking about.

Who knows? Maybe he did.

I stroke his cheek and brush hair out of his eyes. "Of course, Geiger. I'll be right here. You just rest."

Chapter 14

Apparently, pack healing sometimes involves the brothers sleeping together in a sprawling pile of tangled limbs. I understand why Holden is doing it, but I didn't realize that the other brothers had to be in physical contact with Geiger as well.

Maybe they don't. Maybe they're all just too exhausted.

I doze off and on as the time passes, and at some point Holden shifts back into human form. I take that as a good sign.

Holden's stab wound and my cut had taken five hours to heal. Geiger's much more seriously hurt, and after the sixth hour of stroking his hair my stomach starts to rumble. I want to get up and fix myself a snack, but at the same time, I'm afraid of what will happen if I get up. The wolves all want to keep me safe right now, and Matt made it clear earlier that the kitchen was off-limits while there was still a risk that the Mayhem gang might find us.

Rick stirs after the third rumble, and he rubs his sleep-crusted eyes. "You want me to get you something?"

"Would you? Maybe just some chips or something light."

He chuckles and sits up. "With all the noise your stomach's making, you need more than that. I'll see what I can scrounge up."

"Doesn't Holden need you here?"

"Nah, not really. At this point, just being in the house is enough. I'll be back in a few."

I gaze down at Geiger's angular face while Rick goes to fetch me some food, and upon further inspection, it seems like some of his color is back. He's more tan than ghostly white, and there's some pink to his full lips. I trace the outlines of those lips with a fingertip, and Geiger shifts in his sleep. His lips part, tempting me, but I hold back. I'm not about to make out with a sleeping wolf shifter while his brothers are sleeping in the same bed with us. "Later, Geiger. Hold on and get better for now. But later … later I'll spend some time with you."

Ten minutes after he left to make me some food, Rick returns with a tray full of sandwiches, balancing an armful of bottled waters. "Thought I'd get enough for everyone while I was there," he says. "Turkey with mayo on whole wheat okay?"

"It's food, right?" I take one of the sandwiches and bite into it. Whole wheat's not my favorite, but it's not long before I devour the whole thing.

As I eat, Rick wakes each brother in turn and offers them food. Billy and Matt sit up to eat, but Holden shakes his head and stays put. "Geiger's not well enough yet. I need to heal him a little more before he's up to sitting up and eating."

I take one of the bottles of water. "What about this? Surely he needs water."

Holden considers this, then nods. "Just be sure to lift his head enough that he doesn't choke on it."

My instinct is to roll my eyes at him and be a smartass, but instead I behave myself and nudge

Geiger awake to give him some water.

He starts with a few slow sips, but soon he's gulping it down so fast I have to stop him.

"You're going to give yourself an upset stomach if you keep that up," I say. "Take your time."

After he's had enough to drink, Geiger shifts again and tries to sit. Holden keeps him down, but I see that it takes effort on his part. Both men are weak, too weak to fight each other, but Holden's got enough Alpha strength in him to win the argument ... for now, at least.

"I want to sit up," Geiger says.

"Stay put," Holden growls.

"Holden, how long have we been healing?"

Holden looks to me. I glance at my watch again. "About six hours, little more than."

Geiger glares at Holden. "And this poor woman has been holding my head for six fucking hours without a break. Let me sit up so she can go to the bathroom or stretch or something."

"Shit!" Holden sits up and pulls Geiger into a sitting position against his bare chest. "Sorry, Cherry. Why didn't you say something?"

I climb out from under Geiger and slide off the bed. My legs wobble a bit, and I grab the headboard to steady myself. "I didn't even think about it. It wasn't bothering me." I start towards the bathroom, because Geiger made a good point. "And don't lay him back down yet. I'm coming right back."

To my surprise, when I get in the bathroom and glance in the mirror, the hickey from yesterday is gone. I wonder if Holden extended some of his healing magic to that spot while he was at work on Geiger.

When I go back and get comfortable again, Geiger leans against the headboard next to me, using it and my shoulder to prop himself up. His lungs have a slight wheeze when he breathes, which concerns me, but his color is still good.

Holden seems less worried as well. He sits at the other end of the bed and watches us with his ocean blue eyes, and I'm glad he's gotten to where he trusts me enough not to go full wolf whenever I'm near one of his brothers. He still bristles — his muscles still tense whenever he smells one of them on me or sees me touching one of them — but the wolf, at least, stays quiet, hidden behind his human eyes.

Rick and Billy excuse themselves to go change, because their clothes got bloody when they were helping hold Geiger down, but Matt lingers for a few moments. He gazes at me with soulful eyes, and I feel bad that our date ended the way it did. Our sweet and tender turned into blood and terror before we had a chance to enjoy the moment.

I want to go to Matt, to apologize, but what would I say? "Sorry it's my fault your brother got shot half a dozen times. Sorry I endangered your whole family. Sorry I have feelings for more than one of you. Sorry I keep breaking your heart." It all sounds so empty inside my head, and I can only imagine how hollow it would sound to Matt's ears if I voiced the words.

"Hey, Matt." Holden waves him over. "Help me get Geiger back to his own room. I think he's stable enough for that now."

"Sure."

I get out of the way so they can help Geiger to his feet, but I'm determined to stay with him until he's better, so I follow them down the hall to his room. Once they've gotten him situated in his own bed — a queen-sized canopy setup, complete with gauzy curtains — I sit on the bed next to him again and wrap an arm around him.

Matt's eyes flash crystal blue, and I don't miss the whitening of his knuckles.

"I'm going to go for a run. Check the perimeter, check the paths between here and Cherry's grandma's cabin. Make sure no one's around."

Holden locks eyes with Matt. "Be safe, brother."

Matt nods and leaves me alone with the Alpha and his injured Beta wolf.

"Hey, Cherry?"

Geiger's voice surprises me. "Yeah, Geiger?"

He laces his fingers with mine and squeezes my hand. "I'm sorry I fucked up your time with Matt."

"He'll get over it. At least, I hope he will. I mean, I can't leave someone bleeding the fuck out from gunshot wounds they got because of me. Besides, we, uh … we were just about finished."

Holden raises a brow. "Just about?"

A flush heats my cheeks. "Okay, we had finished, but we hadn't planned on ending things there. I mean— Oh, fuck. I can't say anything right."

Geiger chuckles and rests his cheek against my head. "You were basking in the afterglow, and we fucked things up by busting in with me bleeding all over the place. I get it. Don't worry about Matt. Like you said, he'll get over it. He's just the most sensitive of us, so it might take him a little longer."

I look at our linked hands. "I'm sorry I got you shot."

"I don't blame you for that." He gives me a little hug. "I blame Holden. If he hadn't been posturing and goading the Mayhem, I wouldn't have had to jump in front of him to save my Alpha's life."

Holden snorts, and when I look up at Geiger, he's got a wry grin on his face.

"Well, I can see that my immediate work here is done." Holden stretches and turns towards the door. "Now that he's stable, my magic can finish the healing from wherever I am in the house. Just be gentle with him, Cherry. You go ripping open any of those wounds, and I'll have to come right back in here again."

I blink and gape at Holden. "Why would I be ripping open his wounds?"

Holden just laughs as he closes the door.

Geiger nuzzles my neck and whispers in my ear. "Remember when I told you about scents? Right now, you smell possessive whenever anyone gets near me."

"Well, you're hurt." That's a lame excuse.

He chuckles and nibbles on my earlobe. "It's okay. I don't mind. As a Beta, I'm used to being second. I'm just glad I made the list."

"Geiger! Again, I have to remind you that you're hurt. We shouldn't— I mean, Holden's got a point. I could hurt you worse if …" My voice trails off as his teeth nip and nibble their way down my neck to my shoulder. He lets go of my hand and rubs my bare inner thigh. I sigh and shift my hips, spreading my legs a little in a not-so-subtle invitation. "Oh, God, Geiger, that feels so good."

"It's about to feel much better," he murmurs against my skin just before he slides his fingers inside my dripping pussy and rubs my clit with his thumb.

I grind my hips against Geiger's hand and reach for his ready cock with my own hand. I stroke him while he fucks me with his fingers, all fucking four of them, and I come hard and fast in a series of spasms that leave me breathless.

Geiger's not done with me yet, though. He scoots down until he's lying on his back and pulls on my hips. "Come here. Straddle my face. I can't do this right unless I'm lying down. I'm still too weak."

I turn to face the foot of the bed, ready to position myself over him, but he stops me.

"No. Not that way. Don't get me wrong; I'd love a little sixty-nine with you, but I want to look into those beautiful green eyes while I eat that delicious pussy. I want to watch your expression as I drink up your cum."

With a sly grin I take off Holden's shirt and toss it to the floor.

Geiger sucks in a breath as my breasts bounce out, and he reaches up to touch them. His fingertips feel rough and calloused, but when they skip over my taut nipples I shudder at the enticing sensations that rush through me. He takes a heaping handful of each and groans. "God, Cherry, they feel even better than I imagined. So soft and firm." He kneads both breasts for a few seconds, distracted by them, before he remembers why I'm straddling him. "Come here, beautiful."

His hands trail down my sides to my hips and guide me over his mouth. I slide my knees farther apart, inch by inch, teasing, until Geiger pulls my hips with a growl and starts to dig in.

True to his word, he maintains eye contact as he goes down on me. The wolf surfaces in those eyes with their shift from ocean to crystalline blue. He starts slow, licking the cum left over from his thrusting fingers from my slit in long, languid strokes of his tongue. With each lick he shoves his tongue deeper inside me, so deep I worry about his jaw, so deep that I wonder if he's related to Gene Simmons in some way because holy Hell, a human tongue shouldn't be able to do the things he's doing to me right now.

I bite my lip to keep from screaming, because I know if I start that I'll end up throwing my head back in ecstasy, and Geiger wants to see my face. I think he misreads it, though, because he stops and frowns up at me.

"Is something wrong?"

I shake my head. "No, Geiger, it is very, very right. I'm trying to keep eye contact with you, but you've got me seconds away from arching back and screaming into the ceiling."

With a wicked grin, he says, "Well, far be it from me to stop that. You go right ahead." He goes back to work driving me insane, and my back arches until I'm almost bent in half backwards. I put my hands on the bed to keep myself from falling over, and Geiger grabs my hips tighter to hold me to his face.

"Grind me, Cherry. Ride my mouth."

I start to roll my hips, and Geiger growls deep in his throat as he licks me harder and faster, adding suction with his generous mouth to my sensitive clit. I come with a scream, bucking against his face.

Geiger drinks every last drop of me, and when I back off my legs are jelly. Seeing this, he massages my thighs. "Sorry. Was that too much?"

"Don't you *ever* apologize for getting me off so good," I say between gasping breaths.

"So well," he teases, eyes glinting with mischief.

I laugh and swing my leg off him so I can sit down properly. I'd love to climb onto his throbbing hard cock and ride him into next week, but I need a bit of a break first. "A little F.Y.I. for you, Geiger: correcting a woman's post-coital grammar is not as cute as you think it is."

"Maybe I wasn't trying to be cute." He winks. "Now climb back on up here. I'm not done with you yet."

"I can see that," I say with a grin. "I should have brought my water bottle. I need a rest and a drink. All that panting and screaming have me parched."

Geiger points to an ornate cabinet on the far side of the room. "If your legs can make it, there's a fully-stocked liquor cabinet that just happens to have water bottles inside as well." He takes my hand and kisses my palm. "Just get a water for yourself, though. I don't want you getting drunk and ending up even more dehydrated."

"Do you need anything?"

"I need you to get your damn water so we can get back to it. You're torturing me with this waiting."

He's right about my legs. I can barely walk to get to the cabinet and get the water I need. I drink half the bottle in a few thirsty gulps and wipe my chin before stumbling back to the bed. I set the rest of the water on the nightstand after offering it to Geiger, who shakes his head and growls, his wolf eyes hungry for more.

I position myself to give him some head, but he

whines and gently pulls my shoulders towards him, away from his cock. "No. Please, Cherry, no more waiting." His voice, usually so smooth, comes out rough and gravelly. "I've wanted this since I met you. Don't make me wait any more."

I know now how much vulnerability it takes for the wolf to plead, so I nod and swing my leg over his hip. I lower myself in increments, watching his face as I take him into me, inch by inch. Once I've got him all the way inside, I grin and say, "My turn. You'll let me know if I'm hurting you, right?"

He responds with a whine and another growl, and I take that as my signal to just get on with it already.

This is something Eric rarely let me do, because he wanted total control. I've tried it a few times since our breakup, with other guys, but a sudden burst of self-consciousness hits me as I realize that, with Geiger, I actually care if he enjoys it.

Geiger grabs my breasts as I start to raise and lower my hips in a slow, steady rhythm. His grunts and growls encourage me, and I pick up speed, adding a few twists and grinds here and there. Each time I move my hips in a new way, Geiger's eyes flash, and he grips my breasts tighter. Not to the point of pain, but it's definitely a new thing for me to have a guy appreciate my tits the way Geiger does.

As my initial apprehension melts away, I start to enjoy the position for my own benefit. Geiger's dick hits all the right places, and I find that if I grind my hips at just the right point in my movements I can massage that spot deep inside, the spot that drives me wild. My throat mimics Geiger's wild noises as I grunt, groan, and growl.

Beneath me, Geiger matches my movements with pumps of his own. I worry that he'll hurt himself if he does that so soon, but I see no pain in his face, so I keep going.

With Geiger's thrusting added to my own dance, it's not long before my eyes roll back in my head and I arch my spine, screaming Geiger's name as I gush all over his lap. For the third time in two days I'm filled with steamy hot cum, and I hold my hips to his until he gives one last pump.

I want to collapse onto his broad chest, to press my bare breasts that he loves so much against his skin, to let him play with my hair as I recover from it all, but concern over his wounds wins out, and I pull off of him and lie at his side instead.

"How do you feel?" I ask, meaning his injuries.

"Like the luckiest wolf in the world," he says with a sigh.

"I didn't mean that."

Geiger props himself up on an elbow and peels the bandage off the shoulder wound that I had been holding pressure on earlier. As with my stomach, all that's left of the injury is an angry red scar. "Tender, but I'll be fine. Thanks to you."

I give him a hug and nuzzle against his chest, reassured that I won't hurt him in doing so. "I didn't do anything except hold pressure and sit there while Holden and your brothers did all the hard work."

He kisses the top of my head and threads his fingers in my loose waves. "You were there. You could have gone to your room and shied away from the blood and pain, but you stayed with me. That was more help than you know." He sighs. "But I'm not foolish enough to think this means more than it is. You still haven't chosen, have you, Cherry? You still don't know which of us you want."

I sigh as I trace the edge of one bloody bandage with my fingertip. "No, I haven't. I don't know if I even want to choose." I look up into his eyes, which have returned to their human color. "Does that make me a horrible person? I'm not trying to hurt any of you, but I don't want to be hurt, either. If any of you started to lay claim to me, I think I'd have to leave you all."

"Then we'll fight our instincts, Cherry. For you, we'll fight the wolves. Whatever it takes to make you feel safe and happy here."

Chapter 15

I sleep in Geiger's room that night, but the next morning I wake early and slip out to go back to my room for a change of clothes so I can take a shower.

When I get to the guest room, my discarded clothes from my date with Matt—ripped thong and all—are in a pile on the bed. Shit. I pray to whatever God there is that it was Matt who cleaned up after us. If Rick or Billy had the misfortune of taking care of rearranging the living room …

I grab a cute flowery summer dress, some white ankle socks, and some Mary Janes to change into after my shower. I almost opt to go commando with the way my life at the Hunter house has been going, but I throw a pair of underwear on the pile as well.

No cherries in my outfit today, though. That joke is probably getting old, anyway.

I luck out and manage to make it to the big hall bathroom without running into any of the brothers. After my shower, I take some extra time to French braid my wet hair, and I do a quick once-over to make sure I didn't miss any spots shaving my legs. It occurs to me that I haven't really been using lotion since I got here because all I have is scented stuff, so I decide to dig through some of the brothers' drawers to see if they have any unscented lotions. Hell, I'll even take something musky or manly-scented if it means avoiding the hassle of dry, itchy skin.

When Billy comes bursting into the bathroom five minutes later, I've got one leg hiked up on the counter, and I'm in the process of rubbing lotion in. The two of us kind of stare at each other for a moment before Billy turns beet red and backs out of the bathroom, slinging curses and apologies left and right.

"Fuck! Shit, I'm sorry. I forgot we had a guest. Fuck!" He puts a hand over his eyes and turns his back to me.

Poor Billy. "I'm fully dressed, you know. You don't have to turn around."

"Oh, yeah, I kinda do." He clears his throat and shifts his weight, putting his hands on his hips.

I blink and put my leg down, straightening my skirt. "Huh?"

He lets out a huff of air and shakes his head as if to clear it. "I just walked in on you feeling yourself up in a smoking-hot dress. I, uh … Yeah." He looks down then back up and clears his throat again. "I shouldn't turn back around just now."

I can't help it. I burst out laughing. "I'm sorry, but that's too cute. Billy, I wasn't 'feeling myself up.' I was putting lotion on my legs before they got too dry. I don't have any that isn't scented, so I borrowed some from Geiger's drawer."

"Yep. Yeah. Sure." Billy's voice is strained.

I walk up behind him as quietly as I can—for all I know he can hear me anyway, though—and whisper in his ear. "Those tight jeans aren't so comfy now, are they?"

Sure enough, Billy's so distracted that he jumps and yelps when I speak. I double over in laughter as he puts one hand over his crotch and the other over his heart as he turns to face me. "That's not fucking funny." He tries to use a serious tone, but when I look up he's got a wide, toothy grin on his handsome face.

I straighten and pinch his stubbled cheek. "It's hilarious, and you know it. If it had happened to any of your brothers you'd be laughing right on with me."

A growl rumbles from Billy's throat, but his grin stays put, and his irises lighten a couple of shades. "Just because you're absolutely right doesn't mean you can get away with teasing me for it."

"Oh? And what kind of punishment did you have planned for my terrible, terrible transgression?" I lean forward and wink.

Billy's eyes trail downward to zero in on my chest, and his mouth gapes open. "I, uh—"

I close his mouth with a gentle finger under his chin and lift it until his eyes meet mine. "Uh huh. How about you let me get my stuff and get out of your way so you can take care of—" I glance down at the hand over his crotch "—whatever you might need to take care of in here?"

His Adam's apple bobs as he gulps, and I let go. I grab my stuff and leave him with a peck on the cheek and a smack on the ass for good measure.

It's a nice, tight ass. Ten out of ten, no doubt.

On my way to the kitchen for some coffee, I run into Rick. From the glint in his eye and the smirk on his mouth, he overheard my encounter with Billy. I raise my brows and put a hand on my hip. "What's that look for?"

He grins wider. "Oh, you know. I swear, I'm the last guy in this house to have a chance with you, but hearing you hand it to Billy just now almost makes it worth it."

My own grin disappears at his words. "What this about being the last?"

"C'mon, don't play coy. You were flat-out flirting with Billy, and I know you've already been through the others."

Okay, now I'm pissed. I cross my arms over my chest and look him dead in the eye. "'Already been through the others'? So, what, I'm just some wolf shifter groupie? Is that what you think I'm all about?"

Rick turns red, and he stammers through the start of a response, but before I can give him the slap he deserves, Holden walks up behind him and smacks him upside the head so hard he chokes on his words.

"Rick, I don't know what the ever-loving *fuck* is wrong with you, but if I ever catch you talking to Cherry like that again I'll fucking skin your wolf and make a new rug from your hide."

Rick has enough sense to avert his eyes and duck his head in what I recognize as a canine-like submissive pose. Holden snarls and snaps at him, and Rick rushes off down the hall. Holden turns to me and puts a hand on my shoulder. "You okay? That was not cool of him. If you want, I'll go ahead and skin him, anyway."

"And deny me the pleasure?" I say, raising my voice so it carries down the hallway.

Rick's door slams shut, and I smile up at Holden. "I could've done that, you know. You didn't need to come to my rescue."

"I know." Holden takes my chin in his hand and leans in to give me a gentle kiss. "But he needs to fucking learn. These guys aren't used to having a woman here twenty-four seven, and their manners leave something to be desired."

"Yeah, but I feel partly to blame. I mean, Rick and Billy seem so close; I'd hate to cause a rift between them."

"You won't. At least, not a lasting one. Those two are the most twin-like of us. Always together, always in sync. If a rift were to ever form between any or all of us at any point, a serious rift, that is, theirs would mend the fastest." He kisses me again, wrapping his strong arms around me and pulling me close. "I see the healing worked on your neck where I left that mark. Good."

"So you did do that on purpose. I wondered."

"Best way to get rid of it quickly, and more efficient to do it while I'm already healing someone." He grins and winks. "That dress looks amazing on you, by the way." One hand slides down my back to cup my ass.

I stretch up to whisper in Holden's ear. "I don't know if you know this, Holden, but among humans, women who are denied their morning coffee are the most dangerous of the species."

Holden groans and releases me. "Point made."

We head to the kitchen, and just as I'm about to scoop some grounds into the filter, Holden stops me.

"Hold up. I've got a stash."

From the back of the cupboard, he pulls a bag of coffee beans. The label is from an expensive brand, and when he hands it to me I see that it's imported. "Where's the grinder? You're killing me with this stalling."

Holden laughs and grinds up some of the beans for our coffee. While the pot brews, he stands behind me with his hands on my waist and his chin on my head.

His body warms me, and I lean into him. When the coffee's done, he pours us each a mug, and we stand at the kitchen island sipping the aromatic brew.

"What's on the agenda for today?" I ask.

"Geiger, Matt, and I have work. You're stuck with Rick and Billy all day today."

"Cool. Did Matt find anything in his searching last night?"

He heaves a heavy sigh and sets down his mug. "No, and though that should reassure me, I still feel like something's up. I don't think that Westside Mayhem crew is all that bright, but I also don't think they'll just give up on finding you."

"What do you do at your job?"

"What little work I do is part-time. Odds and ends, mostly construction work. Even though I'm an Alpha, I *can* take direction when necessary. Sometimes it's even a little refreshing to not be in charge for once. After you got hurt, I took a couple days off, but I'm needed today."

Coffee's empty. Need more. I pour another mug and inhale the exotic scent. "So the 'twins' are stuck with babysitting duty today."

"Don't put it like that, Cherry. No one here thinks you're a baby, and certainly none of us consider watching you to be 'babysitting duty.'" Holden looks a little hurt by the comment, and for once I avert my eyes. He puts a hand on my bare shoulder and rubs it. It feels nice. "Maybe you guys can do something with your day. Anything in particular you want to do? They could take you shopping, or you guys could take in a movie in an actual theater. Maybe not in town, though. They might have to drive a ways before you get somewhere the cops and the Mayhem dicks won't look for you. But if you're feeling cooped up here, I'll get them to take you somewhere."

I stop to ponder his offer. While I'd like to get out for a bit, I realize the implications. If we go anywhere, Rick and Billy will have to be on high alert for threats to me. They wouldn't enjoy themselves, no matter what we ended up doing. I don't want to do that to them. It's gotta be exhausting, worrying all the time. "We can stay here, unless they have stuff to do elsewhere. I like it here, and besides, I really don't need anything from a store. Geiger brought damn near my whole apartment here when he was there before."

He nods. "Okay. Anything here you want to do? Watch that show you started yesterday, maybe? Go to the family plot and visit your grandma? Whatever the boys can do to make you feel at home, I'll make them do it."

"*Orion's Calling* sounds like a good idea. I was really getting into it."

Just then, Matt stumbles into the kitchen.

"Fucking watching *Orion's Calling* without me," he grumbles as he grabs his own coffee. He takes a sniff and growls. "Hey! What the shit? You never let me brew the good stuff! God, I swear, I bet you'd let me if I grew a pair of tits like that."

Holden raises his hand to give him a smack like Rick got, but I'm faster. "Jerk."

Matt shrinks back. "Sorry. I have an early shift today, and getting up early like this two days in a row is just too much, especially after I was out so late last night."

"Yeah, Holden tells me you didn't find any

evidence that the Mayhem gang knows I'm here. What about Bishop? Do you think he might know where you guys have me?"

"Nah. His scent's all over the burned-down cabin, but it trails off in circles, never even comes close." With a yawn and a stretch Matt checks his watch. "Now, if you'll excuse me, I'm going to head out before I'm late."

Though Holden's standing right there, I give Matt a goodbye kiss on the cheek before he hurries out the door. Holden's not far behind, and when Geiger leaves — looking much better than he did last night — Rick, Billy, and I are sitting together on the couch. Geiger waves at his brothers and blows me a kiss, and just like that I'm alone with the two more submissive of the wolves.

For submissive wolves, when their Alpha and the others aren't around, they sure get bold. Within minutes of the other three leaving, Rick's cozying up behind me on the couch with his arm around my shoulders, holding me close, and Billy's lying with his head in my lap. I guess both brothers have recovered from their earlier teasing and chastising.

Rick trails his fingertips over my bare shoulder and down my arm as Captain Hardigan negotiates with a new alien species for the release of his second-in-command, Commander Biggs. Billy runs his hand up and down my calf, and I have to admit, I can't help but encourage the boys by tangling my fingers in Billy's hair and placing my other hand high on Rick's thigh.

I massage Rick's leg with one hand while the other toys with Billy's hair, my idle fingers in constant movement. Both brothers' muscles tense against me, and from my vantage point, I can see that Billy's getting aroused by it. From the rapid heartbeat behind me and the rock-hard rod pressing against my back, so is Rick.

We sit there, stroking and petting each other, through two full episodes before I start losing track of what's happening on the show. My panties are soaking wet, and I can't concentrate with all the moaning and grunting. I take my hand off Rick's thigh — he groans in complaint — and grab the remote to shut off the TV.

"Why'd you turn it off?" Billy doesn't sound all that disappointed.

"I think we should move to the guest room," I say, breathless.

Rick grins and kisses my neck. "I think we should stay right here. This couch is huge — plenty of room for all three of us."

"Mm, all three, huh?" This just got more interesting.

Billy turns his head and slides my skirt up, exposing my underwear and kissing my thigh. "Rick and I have … let's say different tastes. Tastes that complement each other well."

"What kind of tastes?" I ask, but Rick cuts me off with a kiss. His hand slides under the fabric of my dress to caress my breast, teasing my nipple.

"You'll see."

While he strokes and fondles my chest, Billy nudges my legs open and rolls on his side, facing me. He repositions himself under my leg so his face is right in my crotch, and he pulls my underwear out of his way before diving his tongue inside me. Billy uses his tongue and fingers to drive me to the brink as Rick's massaging hand stimulates my upper body. Rick sucks my tongue into his mouth, covering my screams and moans. His hand joins Billy's at my slit, and I come in jerking spasms.

Unlike his other brothers, Billy doesn't lap up my cum when he's done. Rather, he crawls out from under me and lies back on the couch after stripping out of his clothes, and he strokes himself as he watches Rick continue to finger my pussy, soaking his hand in my juices.

"Turn over." Rick says with a growl. "Get on top of Billy."

I crawl over to Billy until I'm straddling his huge hard-on, and I hear the sounds of a zipper pulling and clothes rustling behind me. Rick flips my skirt onto my back and grabs my panties and yanks, and I've now lost three pair of underwear to the Hunter brothers.

"Fucking clothes in the way," he snarls. His dripping wet hand slides between my cheeks and into my ass. I gasp and arch my back.

So *that's* what they meant by complementing tastes.

I start to inch myself onto Billy's waiting cock, but he thrusts up as soon as the tip enters me, filling me with his girth and burying himself balls-deep inside me. With Rick's slick fingers providing stimulation on a second front, I writhe and scream as Billy pounds my pussy from below. His hands grab my hips while Rick grips my braid with his free hand, and from my vantage point, neither of these boys is a true submissive wolf.

"Now," Rick says into my ear, "this is why I lubed you up first."

When his dick slams into my ass, I cream again.

They don't stop there, though; Billy continues to pump underneath me while Rick fucks my ass, and the twin sensations right on the heels of back-to-back orgasms drive me wild. My back arches even more, and Rick grabs both breasts, pulls them out from my dress, and squeezes, fondling and groping and tweaking and all the good things all at once. I moan, I grunt, I growl, and the boys growl right along with me.

The three of us come together in a chorus of screams, and I'm filled to overflowing.

"Shit! The fucking cushions!" I think of the dumbest shit when I've just had my brains fucked out of me.

Rick gives one last push before sliding out, and he kisses my neck. "They're washable, babe. No worries."

I climb off Billy, gasping for breath, and sit on one of the clean cushions. I don't trust my legs to work just now. Rick squeezes in next to me and rests his sweaty cheek against my breast. Billy's the first of us to regain enough strength to get up.

"Anyone want anything from the kitchen?"

"Water," I say. "Please." Rick nods in affirmation.

Billy disappears into the kitchen, and moments later Rick's whole body tenses against me.

"Did you hear that?" He says it in a whisper, as though he's afraid of being overheard.

My brows knit in confusion. I haven't even heard the fridge open yet. "No, but I'm not part wolf," I say. No sooner are the words out of my mouth than I hear a dull, faint *thud* from the direction of the kitchen.

"Something's wrong," he says, and he stands up, sniffing the air. "Something's very wrong. Cherry, straighten yourself up and run. Book it out the front door, and run as hard and as fast as you can. Don't look back, not for anything. Doesn't matter where you run to; we'll find you later. Just get away."

I don't know what Rick heard before the *thud* or what he smells right now, but a sudden pit develops in the bottom of my stomach. I stuff myself back into my dress, and as soon as everything's in its place I stand and tiptoe towards the front door.

"Don't fucking waste time sneaking," Rick hisses. "Just fucking run." He turns towards the kitchen, hands balled into fists. He creeps through the doorway, and I lose sight of him.

Just as my hand reaches the doorknob, I hear a crash from the kitchen.

Chapter 16

"Just fucking run."

I heed Rick's last words — dear God, I hope they're not his last-last words — and take off out the door at a full run.

Fucking skirt. Fucking cute Mary Janes that are terrible for running in. Fucking forest growing right up to the damn house, with branches snagging and grabbing hold of every bit of loose fabric.

Today's the day I should have worn yoga pants. Or jogging shorts. Some sneakers, maybe a sports bra. I feel fucking ridiculous trying to run for my life in this get-up.

Not to mention I'm not wearing any underwear now.

I skid around the corner of the house and see a driveway, but my bike's not there. I don't know if the Hunters hid it in their garage, but I don't have time to check. There's a car, but I don't know how to hot-wire it.

There's also a familiar motorcycle parked next to the car. Electric blue flames on the bike and sidecar, shiny chrome, huge muffler.

Not my motorcycle. Bishop's.

I turn back towards the thick underbrush and slam into it, running without care to scrapes or scratches or torn clothing.

What was that *thud*? What was the crashing? Is

Billy hurt? Is Rick? I have no idea what's going on. I don't know if Bishop hurt the brothers or if they've got things under control now. Maybe they're running after me right now to tell me everything's okay.

When I hear Bishop's voice shouting my name from back at the house, I know that's not the case.

He did something to Rick and Billy. Hurt them. That's the only way he'd still be alive to come after me. They wouldn't let him walk out that front door to chase me.

Was that the noise Rick heard that I didn't? Did he have a gun with a silencer?

Holden's words echo in my mind. *"Regular bullets will kill us just fucking fine."*

Shit. Billy. Rick.

Hot tears stream down my cheeks as I crash through the trees. I ignore the scratches as the branches whip my face, chest, arms, and legs. I ignore the rips in my dress. I ignore the searing pain in my lungs from overexertion.

"Just fucking run."

When the strap on one of my shoes breaks and I fall on my face, slamming my knee into a sharp rock, I can't help but scream in pain.

"Cherry! I hear you, you fucking bitch. I'll find you! You can't run forever!"

Shit, shit, shit.

I scramble to my feet and limp along. My leg oozes blood from where the rock cut me, and I think I may have twisted something on the way down. My ankle screams with each step, and the whole side of my face hurts.

Now that I'm no longer able to crash through the

trees and brush, now that I'm not making as much noise, I can hear better. The same crashing sounds make their way to my ears, closer by the second, and I know that Bishop hasn't tripped and fallen on his face. He's up and running, full speed by the sound of it, and closing in.

I've got to think. There's gotta be something I can do to get out of this. I try, but I come up blank. The only good thing I can think of, the only pro in this catastrophe of cons, is that my bleeding leg will give Holden and the others a trail to follow.

If they ever come looking for me.

If they're not too busy trying to save Billy and Rick.

If it's not too late for that.

Without warning, the tree next to my head explodes. Well, okay, it doesn't explode—but bits of bark go flying, smacking me in the face, and when I look, there's a bullet lodged in the trunk.

Double shit. I didn't hear the gunshot, which means Bishop does have a silencer.

I duck down low, closer to the level of the underbrush, and keep on moving. I can't stop. If I stop again, I'm dead.

Then I trip again and fall through the bush into a fucking creek. A shallow creek. With more fucking rocks to cut me up. Now I'm bloody all over, and my torn-to-shreds dress is soaked.

This day can't get any worse.

Click-click.

I freeze, half in the water and half out, as I hear the chambering of a round in Bishop's gun.

"There you are, Cherry." Bishop's voice carries enough venom to kill a bull elephant. I lie there, waiting to die, but instead I hear footsteps moving closer.

"I can't believe you did this to Eric. Breaking up with him was bad enough, cheating on him was worse, getting him arrested for giving you what you fucking deserved, then you fucking killed him and burned down your own grandma's cabin to cover it up? And if all *that* wasn't reason enough to kill your ass, I find you out here shacking up with five guys." He chuckles, but it's not a mirthful sound. "Yeah, I've been watching this place all day. I saw three of 'em leave, and I snuck in while you were screwing the other two back in the house up there. You three were so fucking loud you didn't hear me break in, so distracted that none of you saw me watching you."

By now he's caught up to me, and I hear splashing as he steps into the creek. He crouches just at the edge of my vision, gun barrel in front of my face. "I watched you cheat on my dead brother, you fucking whore. I watched you take two fucking dicks at once. While my brother lies on a slab in the fucking morgue!" Bishop pushes the gun against my forehead to punctuate his rant, and I can't help the sob that escapes me.

"That's right, cry like the bitch you are. Go ahead; piss yourself, if you have to. You and me, we're gonna spend some quality time together. I'm gonna teach you how to act. No more of this slut bullshit. No more fucking around. You've sucked and fucked your last pretty boys, Cherry. Hope it was worth your miserable life."

"Please, Bishop. Please don't kill me." It hurts my face to cry, but since just about everything hurts at this point, and I'm half naked in a creek, I go ahead and bawl.

Bishop tucks the gun barrel under my chin and uses it to lift my head so I'm looking up at him. He's six feet of what I used to think was solid muscle. Now that I've had all five Hunter brothers as comparisons, I realize that he's just got a moderately decent body for a guy who hits the gym every day. His off-the-wall flash tattoo sleeves seem bland and uninspired, and his brown hipster beard and slicked-back hair just look pathetic. I'm not about to vocalize my comparisons, though. Not with a gun on me.

I used to think Eric's brother was kinda cute. Guess I've been spoiled by the Hunters.

"Oh, I'm not going to kill you just yet. You've gotta suffer for your sins, Cherry." He reels his arm back and pistol-whips me in the forehead, hitting me so hard the other side of my head slams into a rock beneath me. My vision splits into two images that slide back and forth, overlapping then splitting then overlapping again. The stars at the edge of my vision linger, and my stomach reels. A high-pitched ringing squeals in my ears.

Bishop yanks my arms behind me and ties them tight with something — I think maybe a zip tie. My legs get the same rough treatment, and I scream in pain as he grabs me around the waist and hauls me up, tossing me over his shoulder like a sack of flour. I think I broke something when I fell in the creek. It shouldn't hurt this much.

More tree branches whip me as he stomps through the woods back to his motorcycle. Now that I'm closer to him, I smell the liquor on his breath. That worries me. He's never been the most in-control kind of guy; add drunk and mourning into the mix, and I'm in deep shit.

"Bishop, please, don't do this." I'm at the bargaining phase of my impending death, trying to reason with a madman. "You're never going to get far. Once you get on the highway, someone's going to notice you've got a trussed-up, half-naked, beat-to-shit woman on your motorcycle. They'll call the cops, and you'll be arrested."

"No one's going to see shit. I brought the sidecar, so as far as anyone knows you're just a fucking sack of laundry."

Crap. I forgot about the sidecar. If he does put me in a sack, at high enough speeds no one's going to think twice about what—or who—is in the sack.

If Holden hasn't sensed Rick and Billy's injuries through the pack bond by now, I'm screwed. As it is, not enough time has passed between now and the gunshots back at the house for him to make it back from town to check on his brothers and me. I wasn't running very long before I fell, and Bishop's moving like he's a man on a mission.

I guess he is.

A mission to torture and kill me.

I scream again when Bishop dumps me in the sidecar. Something is definitely broken. He stuffs a rag in my mouth and ties it with another scrap of fabric. Bishop came prepared.

When he shoves the sack over me, the world goes quiet for a moment. All that's left is the ringing in my ears.

Then the bike's engine turns over, and I have to endure the bumpy back roads leading into town. Bishop's not taking any of the roads easy, and I'd almost swear he's hitting the rocks and potholes on purpose just to hear more of my muffled screams.

I try to assess where the pain is coming from, but I'm so badly hurt it's almost impossible to tell. My knee and ankle for sure, possibly some ribs, and of course my throbbing head — and that's not mentioning the sting of dozens of cuts and scratches from my run through the trees. The rough canvas of the sack abrades my torn skin, but I'm grateful for the cover. By the time Bishop deposited me in the sidecar, I had mere shreds of a skirt, and only one boob was covered.

If I survive this, I'll have to charge the Hunters for the losses to my wardrobe.

Shit, the Hunters. Rick and Billy could be dying, or already dead by now, and even if Holden catches my scent in the woods outside their house — and between sex with his brothers, the blood, and my own fear and sweat, he's going to smell my trail through the trees — I'm pretty sure this motorcycle ride will be enough to lose even the wolves.

No one's going to come for me.

I try to do like I've seen on crime dramas, where they listen for things like train horns or other sounds to give the cops clues on how to find them, but I can't hear anything over the bike mufflers and the incessant ringing. I worry that Bishop did some real damage when he hit me with the gun.

Not like I'll be alive long enough for it to matter.

After an eternity of bumpy back roads, Bishop pulls onto the highway. I'm so out of it that I can't even tell if he turned left or right, so I have no clue where we're headed, but I'm grateful for the smoother ride.

Another I-don't-know-how-many-minutes later,

the engine sounds get louder, like more motorcycles have joined us. It's at this point that I realize just how screwed I truly am.

Chapter 17

I didn't put the pieces together before, but Bishop rides a bike, owns guns, has access to a silencer.

He's in the Mayhem.

Like, deep in. Deeper than Eric was. No *wonder* they've been snooping around my apartment, and it's probably also why they shot Geiger. They wouldn't do it just for Eric's sake, but if Bishop's in as deep as I suspect, it makes sense.

I should have paid more attention when I was dating Eric, but I didn't want to get involved. Besides, if I even looked at Bishop — or any man — sideways, Eric assumed I was flirting and got violent with me. So yeah, I never noticed if any of his tats were Mayhem symbols, or if he had a Mayhem jacket, or anything like that. I was too busy keeping my head down and my eyes to myself.

Between the blows dealt by Bishop, the ringing in my ears, and the roar of the motorcycles, my head throbs. I'd kill for some over-the-counter painkillers right now. Hell, with as beaten up as I am, I'd kill for some oxy.

Maybe someone from the Mayhem will take pity on me and give me a few before they blow my brains out.

I hope the worst they do to me is blow my brains out.

Oh, God, what if they do something worse?

It occurs to me that I'm beaten halfway to hell, almost naked, and zip-tied. They could do whatever sick thing they wanted, and I couldn't do a thing to stop them.

Please, Holden — Geiger, Matt, anyone — please come find me. Please hurry.

And please, don't let Rick and Billy die, either.

Oh, crap; Holden's going to have to choose between saving them or saving me. What the hell kind of mess have I gotten them into?

The engine sounds wane, and the motorcycle slows. After a few turns on what must be side streets with lower speed limits, the bike comes to a stop and idles for a second before Bishop cuts the engine.

I take a deep breath to steady myself after the ride and regret it immediately. There's no question; I did something to my ribs when I fell. I cry out in pain, and something hits my head.

"Shut the fuck up, whore!"

Not Bishop's voice. Another gang member. That tells me a couple of things: for one, there are at least two armed men here with me, and two, no one has any compunctions about hurting me.

Panic seeps in through the cracks in my addled mind, and I realize there's no way anyone can save me in time.

Rough hands haul me out of the sidecar, and I grit my teeth to stop myself from screaming again and earning another punch. Good behavior has its own downside, though; whoever's got me has grabby hands, and even through the thick sack they grope and fondle. My stomach churns, and I wish they'd go back to hitting me.

My mystery carrier deposits me on a hard surface without any care to my comfort or safety, and I swear to God, I'm so sick of screaming, but I can't help it this time. I land square on my side, right on my injured ribcage, and my voice breaks. I receive a kick in those same ribs as a reward. With no strength left in my lungs to scream again, I moan and roll to the other side. Someone yanks and tugs at the sack until it's off me, and a chorus of raucous laughter greets me when I'm exposed.

More than two armed men, then, and a lot more by the sound of it.

Instinct takes over, and I clamp my knees together and roll into the tightest ball I can. My ribs protest, but any amount of pain is better than what these assholes might do if they get a good view of me naked.

It's a futile attempt. They chase the laughter with hoots, hollers, and wolf whistles. Crude comments fly in the commotion, slithering past the ringing in my ears. No less than five different voices that I can pick out go into excruciating detail about what they plan to do to me when it's their "turn."

None of it sounds pleasant.

Bishop's voice booms at them to shut up, almost echoing in my head, and the din calms.

An ice-cold chill runs down my spine as I realize why none of the gang members ever tried anything with me when I was dating Eric. It never had anything to do with Eric's control over me. It never had anything to do with any kind of good graces he had with the gang. It was never about Eric at all.

This whole time, I didn't know how lucky I had been to only get beaten and controlled by one man.

Now, with their leader, Bishop, holding my short future in his cruel hands, I fear I'm about to find out how much worse things could have been.

Steel-toed boots clomp towards me on the hard floor—concrete, from the feel of it underneath my skin. A hand grabs my braid and yanks my head up, and I'm face-to-face with Bishop. A solid dozen bikers with guns lounge in a rough semicircle behind him, sitting on boxes and pallets. Empty booze bottles litter the ground in what I now recognize as a warehouse.

There are scores of warehouses downtown, both used and abandoned. I could be just about anywhere in a thirty-mile radius.

Bishop's brown eyes bore into mine, and he spits in my face. The gang behind him laughs when I flinch.

"I don't know what Eric ever saw in you. From what he told me, you never fucking learned how to behave. Always flirting with customers at the bar, running around behind his back. You may have a tight ass and some nice tits, but I can't imagine any pussy could be good enough to put up with the shit you put him through."

So this is where Eric got the crazy ideas about owning me. He learned it from his brother.

I think back on the past two or three days, the best days of my life, really. Even when Geiger was hurt, even when I was dying, my time with the Hunter men surpassed anything else I'd been through in my shitty existence. What kind of life would I have had if I'd known that men could be so loving and kind, without any need to stoke their fragile egos?

I might have been bolder, braver. I might not have been the pushover that Eric made me into.

Then I remember Holden's words:

"You would literally be incapable of looking my wolf in the eye if you were at all as submissive as you're trying to make yourself out to be."

That's right; I'm not a sub. I'm a dominant wolf. I mean, not a literal wolf like the Hunter brothers can be, but I'm strong in my own right. I can get out of this, somehow, if I just focus on that strength.

"That's something you have to dom up and do yourself."

Holden's words steel me against the strain in my neck from the way Bishop's holding my hair. They tamp down on the pain coursing through my battered body. They cut through the incessant ringing in my ears. They embolden me.

I'm about to do something really stupid, but damned if I'm not going to go down swinging.

Metaphorically swinging, that is … unless this works.

Bishop tied my gag plenty tight, but I still glare at him and try to mumble around it.

"What's the matter, cunt? Cat got your tongue?" He laughs at his own joke as he pulls the gag off and tosses it to the side. "I suppose I can give you the dignity of having some last words before me and my boys wreck that pussy of yours." He licks his lips and adjusts his crotch with his free hand.

Fucking pervert.

"See, that's your problem, Bishop. You think it's all about the pussy. I've got so many more things I can do with my hands and legs and mouth that you couldn't even dream of in that tiny little nugget you Neanderthals call a brain."

"Fucking bitch!" He twists my braid, but I grit my

teeth and bear it. I even give him a smile.

This is something I have to dom up and do myself. Holden's got his brothers to tend to. No one's getting me out of this but me.

"I mean, look at this. You're so fucking insecure that, even with me beat to shit, you think you need to tie me up to control me. That's just sad. Pathetic, really. What grown-ass man is afraid of a woman who's five inches shorter than him and a buck thirty soaking wet?"

That one earns me the prize of having my head slammed into the concrete. I feel a crunching in my nose, which starts gushing coppery-smelling blood.

I force myself to laugh through the pain.

"Shit, you don't even have the balls to hit me yourself. Let the floor do all the fucking work for you." I roll my shoulders and shift until I'm in a more comfortable position, for whatever that's worth at this point. "I bet you wouldn't know what the fuck to do with me if I didn't have a pussy. All you know how to do is bark orders and rut like a fucking dog. No imagination, no courage—just a fucking animal."

Bishop snarls, and I reply by spitting blood in his face. He lets go of my head, but to my relief he doesn't do further brain damage this time.

Gotta keep going. Can't stop now. I've poked the beast, and if I don't keep poking, it's going to sense weakness.

I don't have weakness. I am dominant.

I'm a fucking Alpha female, and he's going to learn what that means.

"Man up, Bishop. Put your balls where your mouth is. Cut these fucking ties, and we'll go. You and me." I watch the confusion cross his face in the knitting of his brows and gape of his jaw. He probably thinks I've lost my ever-loving shit.

Good. Let him think that.

"What? Are you scared? Afraid of a beaten little girl? Shit, you're probably wetting your pants right now because your baby brother isn't here to boss me around anymore. Can't hide behind him like you used to, now that he's burnt to a fucking crisp."

From the reactions in the peanut gallery, Bishop's not the only one baffled by my shit talk. Most of the rest of the gang has fallen silent, and they exchange incredulous looks. Some of their faces even show doubt. Now that the ringing has stopped, I hear some of their whispers.

"Why *doesn't* he untie her?"

"Eric *was* always the one in charge of her, now that I think about it."

"He wouldn't even let us have a turn while Eric was alive. We *always* get our turn with the bitches, except this one."

Encouraged by the slight shift in power, I keep going. "C'mon, Bish. Cut these ties. Or are you really that scared of me?"

Bishop reaches back and pulls out a foot-long serrated knife—much like the one Eric almost killed me with a few days ago. His face burns beet-red, and the veins in his neck and biceps bulge.

"I'll show you how fucking scared I am."

Chapter 18

The blade of the knife flashes in the fluorescent warehouse lights, but I don't flinch when he brings it swinging down.

He's rough with it, and in the process of cutting my zip ties he nicks my arms and legs both. The smell of fresh blood strengthens, and with it I notice other, new smells. Sweat and sex, yes, that makes sense after the morning I've had, but something rancid hits my nostrils as well, something visceral that reminds me of fear and terror.

C'mon, Cherry, focus. Can't be distracted by weird olfactory hallucinations. Plan A worked. Now on to Plan B.

I just gotta figure out what Plan B is.

Well, Step One has to be getting the fuck off the floor. Can't go posturing that I'm this badass and then lie there like a ragdoll.

This time, Rick's voice echoes in my mind, coaxing me to keep going.

"You'd totally rival Holden for Alpha status if you were one of us."

That's right. I'm the Alpha female.

It hurts like a motherfucker, but inch by inch, bit by painful bit, I get from the floor to a standing position without making a sound. I don't cry when an agonizing pain shoots from my ankle all the way up to my hip. I don't scream when my ribs revolt against the increased movement. I don't whimper when I wipe my bloody broken nose.

I just stand there like the fucking War Goddess that I am, and I stare Bishop right in the eye.

"Now give me the fucking knife, you pencil-dicked asshole." I hold out my hand, palm up, and wiggle my fingers in the universal sign for "gimme."

When this is over, I'm going to need a head CT. Maybe an MRI. And a full psych eval.

The gathered bikers burst into laughter, and Bishop's face goes from red to a hideous shade of purple. "I'm not giving you a fucking knife, you twat."

"So you're too scared to face me man-to-woman? Need your guns and knives to feel powerful, do you?" I shrug and cross my arms over my half-bare chest. "All right. I'm game. I mean, it doesn't look all that great to your crew over there if you don't get rid of the thing, but who am I to judge?"

Bishop growls, but it's not like the growls of the wolves. It's a weak growl, a human growl, a growl of desperation, and I smirk in response.

He raises the knife, but instead of plunging it into me, he buries the entire blade in a crate next to him. His hands scramble to rid himself of the four guns he has on his person — which was three guns more than the one I remembered him having.

Then he starts removing his clothes, and I almost lose my cool. What the hell is he doing?

"Well?" he says as he wiggles his half-limp dick free of his briefs, the last of his clothing to go. He's even got his boots off. "You're all talk, but are *you* going to face *me* on an even field? No weapons, no clothes, just you versus me." He grins and grabs the floppy member at his crotch to wave it at me. I think it's intended to intimidate me.

It's not working.

Without removing my gaze from his eyes, I tear the remnants of my dress off and take off my shoes and socks, one at a time. When I get to my twisted ankle, I bite my tongue against the shooting agony that comes with pulling my Mary Jane off the swollen foot. I school my expression to remain calm, stoic, bitchy even. The sock, at least, gives me less pain with its removal.

Here it is. The moment where I learn what a fucking brain-damaged idiot I am. Alpha personality or no, I don't stand a chance against Bishop. Not in a one-on-one fight. Not in any fight.

Out of the corner of my eye, I see Bishop grab his dick with his other hand, too, and it's difficult to tell without breaking my Alpha stare, but I think he's trying to work himself hard.

The fucking dumbass.

When Bishop stabbed the crate, he stabbed it within reach of me. He stabbed it right at neck-height for him.

He stabbed it with the sharp edge facing him.

As soon as both of his hands are occupied, as soon as I see my opening, I grab the handle of his knife and jerk it free of the crate. I use the momentum of the knife sliding loose to continue the arc of my arms, bringing the blade across his neck in an elegant swipe that opens his throat and sends arterial spray pulsing out. I allow myself the freedom to close my eyes and tilt my head back, arms spread wide, bathing my nude body in the death of the family that caused me so much pain, physical and emotional. The acrid stench of copper fills my nostrils, though it's a different copper than my own blood. Strange.

Bishop falls to the floor with a wet *thud*.

Plan B accomplished, thanks to some improvisation. Now on to Plan C.

Unfortunately, Plan C involves getting past the rest of the Mayhem.

I didn't make them give up their weapons. I may have a knife, but all it'll take is one well-aimed shot to drop me right where I stand. Hell, they may fill me with bullets just for playing dirty with the whole knife thing.

To my complete and utter surprise, no one shoots me.

Keeping with the Alpha act—although it feels less and less like an act—I open my eyes and swivel my head to glare at the gang members in the warehouse. To a man, they set their guns down with haste and back up, arms up and eyes wide.

Once again, their whispers reach my ears.

"She's fucking crazy!"

"Dude, look at her fucking eyes…"

"Weren't they green a second ago?"

"It's like they're fucking glowing…"

I don't know what the fuck they're talking about, and maybe I'm hallucinating again, but their actions say all I need to hear. The Mayhem is scared shitless by my insane actions, and when I take a step in their direction and growl for effect, they scramble to the exit. Within seconds, I hear the sounds of bike engines revving and tires squealing.

I think I smell a little lingering piss, and gross as that may be, I smile at the thought that I scared them that badly.

The warehouse lies empty, devoid of human life except for a lone blood-drenched woman.

I did it. I fucking did it.

Unfortunately, without my act holding me together, my nerves of steel start to unravel. I drop the knife with a clatter, and my body trembles. Tears stream down my battered, blood-covered cheeks, and I wipe a mixture of blood and snot from my nose. This time, I allow myself a sharp intake of breath at the flash of pain that explodes in my face when I touch the broken bone.

I lower myself to the floor and sit in the pool of Bishop's blood. I've exhausted all my physical and mental reserves, and it's all I can do to sit upright — and that's using the crate to my side as a prop. My worn body screams at me to lie down, to succumb to the aches and pains and just drift off to one last sleep.

Then I hear an engine approach outside.

It's not a motorcycle engine; too clean, too quiet. Did the Mayhem bring a car or van to come back for Bishop's body? If they did, I'm screwed. I don't have it in me to keep up the charade.

Still, I can't just give up. Not now. I reach down and wrap my fingers around the handle of the knife, gripping it tight. They'll have to shoot me. If they even try to get close without killing me first, I'll take down as many of them as I can before they overwhelm me. I owe it to Holden and Rick and Billy, to Geiger and Matt. I owe it to them all, to the wolves who cultivated the Alpha inside me, to go down fighting, despite how tired I might be.

As the car doors open — no, wait, it must be a van,

because I hear a sliding door — I force my aching body into a defensive crouch.

I don't know if it's the head injuries, but the sounds that reach my ears seem magnified. I hear hushed whispers outside, when I shouldn't hear anything at all from in here. I hear the creak of the van's carriage as one — no, two bodies exit the vehicle.

I hear Holden's deep, rumbling, growling voice, and fresh tears spring to my eyes, tears that have nothing to do with the pain I'm in.

"Yes, I'm fucking certain she's in there. Be careful; she's badly injured. She feels almost feral. Now go! I don't know how outnumbered we are, but we've got to get her back. I'll stay with Rick and Billy in here and keep healing while you get her."

Relief floods my fried system when Geiger's massive form comes through the warehouse door. He moves slow at first, but once his eyes meet mine, he whines and takes off at a full run. Matt isn't far behind him, and both men's wolves shine at the forefront in their glowing crystal-blue eyes, like twins sets of bright blue beacons.

Geiger kneels in front of me, just out of reach, and breaks eye contact to assess the bloody mess that is my body. "Cherry? Are you okay? There's so much blood, I can't tell where Bishop's ends and yours starts."

"It's mostly his."

Matt skids to a stop, and when I shift my eyes to meet his, he gapes in shock and looks at his brother. "Is that —"

Yeah," Geiger says, still avoiding eye contact with me. "I can't believe it, either. I thought Holden had lost his fucking mind when he said he could sense her through the pack bond."

"I thought that was just some old wolves' tale."

Geiger sighs. "Me, too. Guess those old wolves knew what they were talking about."

I look back and forth between the two men, dumbfounded. "What are you guys going on about? What old wolves' tale?"

"Never mind that now. Are you able to walk?"

I shake my head. "I'm fucking spent. My ankle's hurt, my ribs are hurt, my nose is broken, and I've been hit in the head at least four times. I think the only thing that's kept me going this far is a combination of adrenaline and bullheadedness."

Geiger nods. "Okay. If you'll allow it, I'll carry you back to our van. Holden's in there with Rick and Billy." A canid whine escapes my throat, and Geiger holds his hands out. "They're hurt, but they'll be okay. We got to them in time. Holden's already started healing them."

Thank God. "Okay. Yeah, you can pick me up, just be cautious with the ribs. I can't tell, but I think some of them are broken."

If I wasn't at the end of my, well, everything, I might have the energy to be amazed at how gentle Geiger is with me. He picks me up like I'm made of spun glass, like the slightest bit of jostling could shatter me.

Who knows? Maybe it would.

Strange smells assault my nostrils the closer we get to the van, and I wonder what kind of product this warehouse held. Whatever it is, or was, it smells like … like pain, I guess, would be how I'd describe it. Pain, but also fear and love. Weird.

That reminds me of my need for medical imaging

of my beaten brain.

When Geiger puts me in the van, Holden's already shifted into wolf form. He's lying across Rick and Billy, who have been stripped naked and placed on some blankets and pillows in a makeshift bed on the floor of the van. The two brothers have matching bloody bandages on their chests, but from the location and the amount of blood, it appears that Bishop isn't as good a shot as he thought he was. Geiger tries to situate me so I'm in physical contact with the dogpile, but I push his hands away.

"No. Holden needs to heal them first. I can wait."

Geiger sighs and pinches the bridge of his nose. "Typical Alpha," he mumbles, and he throws his hands up in the air. "Well, Holden? I can't just disobey her. We're kind of at an impasse here, unless you override her. I'll give you seniority on this, at least for now."

Holden replies in a mixture of wolfish growling and human speech that echoes in my aching head.

Huh? I didn't know he could speak when he was a wolf.

"Damnit, Cherry, you need healing, too. Just let us help you."

I reply with some growling speech of my own. "No. Heal them first. They need it more. I can hold on until we get to a human hospital or something."

Holden's whine turns into another growl, but he lays his head back down on Rick's bloody chest. "This is a terrible time to decide to assert yourself, Cherry. Fine. We won't force you to accept my healing—yet. But we can't take you to a hospital, either. We'll take you back to the house. To my room. We need the whole pack together tonight."

Satisfied that I won this argument, I lean my head back against the wall of the van and sniff the air. The stench of pain is fetid, and the fear smells noxious, but the scent of love permeates the interior of the van like a sweet perfume, and that's the part I focus on. I'm going to miss this when the swelling in my brain goes down.

A light buzzing tickles my nerve endings, and Matt sits next to me while Geiger takes the wheel. I nuzzle my head into Matt's neck and use him as a kind of cushion against the van's poor shocks. Even on the city streets, before we get to the back roads to the house, the jostling hurts. The weird buzzing helps a little, but I'll be glad to get in Holden's plush bed and snuggle down with the pack.

My pack.

It hits me just then that I've accepted them as my own, just as much as they've accepted me. Not in a sense of claiming, but in a sense of family. Of togetherness.

I could get used to this feeling.

Chapter 19

I grit my teeth through the bumpy return trip to the Hunter house, and when the pain gets bad enough to elicit some small whines and whimpers from me, Matt wraps an arm around my shoulders and holds me close.

"We're almost there, Cherry. Just hang on."

I nod my heavy head and almost—*almost*—allow myself to slip out of consciousness. If Rick and Billy weren't still hurt, I might have let the darkness take me, but I can't. Not when my pack needs me.

When we get home, the spectacle of getting me and the two injured wolves into the house from the garage makes me giggle. Matt carries me in first, despite my feeble attempt at asserting myself, and Geiger carries Rick and Billy in much like Bishop carried me through the woods earlier, minus the zip ties. Holden trots along behind us on all fours, tongue lolling out, tail wagging.

Matt lays me down in the middle of Holden's bed, and Rick and Billy are placed on either side of me. I remember an earlier time, just today but it feels like forever ago, when I was part of an entirely different kind of Rick-and-Billy sandwich.

Holden jumps up on the bed and sprawls across the three of us, and it surprises me that his weight doesn't crush me or hurt my ribs. The buzzing intensifies, and some of my pain fades.

"Cherry." Holden's voice echoes in my head again. Maybe when he heals me, he can take care of this damned annoying brain damage while he's at it. "I need your help with this."

I scratch behind his ears, more for my comfort than his. I'm getting tired. "What can I do?"

"You feel that hum, that vibration throughout your body?"

"Mm-hmm." Sure I do. It's another hallucination. I don't know how the fuck Holden knows about it, but whatever. I'm open to anything right now.

"I need you to hum, too, Cherry. We need to hum together to heal you three faster."

I start to hum a little nonsense song in the back of my throat, but Holden yips.

"No, not like that. Reach inside you and hum from inside, from the core where you feel it."

He's not making any sense, but neither is anything about this day, so I give it a shot. I close my eyes and focus on the sensation of the buzz, or the hum as he calls it, that rides my nerves and zeroes in on all the broken parts of me. Something about the hum resonates inside me, and to my surprise an answering hum, similar but unique, reverberates from deep within. The two vibrations harmonize in a melody that's beyond sound, beyond anything I've ever heard or felt.

It's absolutely fucking beautiful.

My lids grow heavy, and I know I won't be able to fight sleep much longer. "Hey, Holden, do I have to stay awake to hum?"

He licks my chin and whines. "No. Sleep, Cherry. Rest. The Alpha magic knows what to do."

"M'kay." That's all the permission I need.

*   *   *

Healing comas are nice. I never really appreciated the one I was in before, when Holden saved my life the first time a few days ago. It's like the best nap ever, combined with a spa treatment, mixed with a few margaritas' worth of relaxation.

I wake alone in Holden's bed, with a hushed argument echoing in my ears. Did the healing not fix my brain damage? I open my eyes to see who's in the room with me, but I'm alone in the room, too. The door's open, though; maybe I'm hearing them out in the hallway.

"You've got to be the one to tell her, Holden." Geiger. The voice of reason.

Holden groans. It's loud but distant at the same time. "I know, I know. It's just— How do I explain this? It's damn near unheard of, and even then I thought it was just a legend. It hasn't happened in recent memory of any wolf I've talked to, not since our grandparents' grandparents were little kids on *their* grandparents' knee."

Matt's voice chimes in. "But it *has* happened before?"

"In fairy tales!" Holden smells agitated. Why does he smell agitated—and why do I know that's what that smell is?

Fuck, the healing *didn't* fix my brain damage. I'm still smelling weird shit and hearing more than I should. Is this conversation even really going on?

Maybe I'm still in the coma.

"What does this mean for us? Y'know, as a pack." Billy. That voice and the scent that wafts with it is Billy.

He smells less like pain now, which is good, but more like … hm, not sure how to articulate it. I inhale deep, take a bigger whiff, and let the scent roll around in my nostrils for a bit. Anxiety? Yeah, that must be it. On the edge of fear, but less acrid.

Geiger speaks up again. "Alpha couples aren't uncommon in packs, but I think we all know that Cherry doesn't want to be part of a couple. So, I guess the question to Holden would be this: Are you willing to let another Alpha stay in your pack if she's not yours and yours alone?"

Holden sighs, bringing the scent of something cloudy and murky to my nose. Grief? Sorrow? Maybe, but that doesn't make sense. "A better question might be 'Would Cherry want to stay in a pack where she's not the only Alpha?'"

Okay, that's two Cherries in a conversation where I'm not in the room. Time to haul my ass out of bed and go find out what's up.

I breathe a sigh of relief when I stand up and nothing hurts. Looking down at my naked body, I seem to be all in one piece. No bruising or swelling, and I bet if I checked underneath the bandage on my knee, the cut will be gone.

A quick scan of the room reveals that someone — likely Geiger — laid out some of my clothes for when I woke up … and by "laid out some of my clothes," I mean he set an entire drawer from my dresser on a chair off to the side. I grab a baby-doll tee and some track shorts and throw them on before heading towards the sounds and smells of the Hunter brothers. I don't even bother to check my hair in Holden's bathroom.

I waltz into the great room, and five heads turn to

stare at me. I lean against the wall and make a show of examining my fingernails, like I'm checking for dirt under them or something. There's not any, of course; someone cleaned me up pretty good while I was out.

Act casual, Cherry. "So, what's all this crap about a legend and two Alphas?"

Four pairs of eyes look away from mine when I glance back up. Holden meets my gaze.

"How are you feeling, Cherry?"

"Uh-uh. No deflecting. Out with it."

He sighs and stands up. "I'm not deflecting. I need to know how you feel right now. Are you healed? Any pain? Discomfort?"

I shake my head. "No, but I think I need to get my brain checked out. At a human hospital. Ever since Bishop beat the snot out of me, I've been hearing and smelling weird things. Like, you guys sounded super loud when I woke up, even though I was down the hall. And the olfactory hallucinations are a bit annoying."

"Those aren't hallucinations, Cherry."

I snort-laugh and roll my eyes. "C'mon, only you wolves can smell feelings and shit like that."

"Well, there are some other non-human races out there that can, too. Fae folk, for instance, or demons, or—"

Holden growls. "Geiger, now is not the time."

I wave an arm in Geiger's direction. "Thank you, Geiger. My point exactly. I'm not a non-human. I'm as human as you can get. One hundred percent, bona fide human."

The room falls silent, and the cloying, edgy scent of anxiety threatens to suffocate me.

"What? What the fuck is going on?"

Holden takes a couple steps towards me, cautious steps, like he's approaching a wild animal. "Here's the thing, Cherry: We don't think you're one hundred percent human anymore."

My upper lip curls, and I growl.

It's not the cutesy little human woman pretend growl I'm used to hearing from my throat.

The sound that comes out of me is raw. Primal. Feral. *Animal.*

Matt and Geiger don't react, but Holden, Rick, and Billy all gasp. Geiger runs a hand through his hair and lets out a huff of air that smells like … resignation? "Told you. Just like at the warehouse."

Matt nods in affirmation.

"What? What is 'just like at the warehouse'?" I sweep the room with my gaze, but only Holden meets my eyes. "What the shit is going on? Why won't you guys look at me? You're all acting like I'm Holden on a rampage."

"They're showing submission, Cherry. I've told you before that you're a dominant personality; right now, your wolf is showing in your eyes, and they're submitting to the wolf. This is nothing new to you, really; you've seen this behavior plenty of times since you've been here."

That's it. I'm sick of this cryptic bullshit. "What do you mean my wolf is showing in my eyes? I don't *have* a wolf!"

Holden sighs and takes my shoulders in his hands. He marches me out of the room and to the hall bathroom. Once in front of the mirrors, he turns me to face one of them and holds me there, like he's afraid

I'm going to bolt if he lets go.

Seeing the crystalline blue irises in my eyes, the color I've come to associate with the brothers' wolves surfacing, he might be right. I might just run for the hills. Like, right now.

"How?"

Holden's eyes shift behind me in the mirror, and he wraps his skull-covered arms around me. "That's what all that 'crap about a legend' was about." He kisses the top of my head. "I had to call around to some other packs to verify, because it's been so long since my grandmother told me the story, but there's a legend among us wolves that, until today, I thought was pure myth.

"It's said that, long ago, there was a human woman who fell in love with a wolf. She longed to be part of the pack, but the pack rejected her because she wasn't a wolf herself. So she visited her wolf lover every night in secret, and, in time, she became a wolf. She became pack through her connection to him."

My face in the mirror frowns. "So … werewolfism is, like, an STD?"

"It's called lycanthropy, not werewolfism. And that's an oversimplification. Besides, we're not lycanthropes. We're shifters; we're born this way, remember? We don't transmit anything, don't change people with a bite. There's no virus in your system, no disease. You're not sick, Cherry. There's nothing wrong with you. You're just … different. Our pack magic changed you. You're no longer human."

"I'm a wolf."

"Yeah."

I turn in his arms to look in his crystal-blue eyes.

"Can I shift?"

"I don't know. You know just about as much as I do right now." He tips my chin up with a finger and leans down to give me a gentle kiss. "Your life has changed, Cherry. You're not human anymore. You can't go back to your old life. Well, I mean, you're wanted for Eric and Bishop's murders, for one thing, but that aside, living with humans is difficult for us. Our instincts take over, and as an Alpha you'll want to dominate or protect almost every human you meet. Your wolf will see them as weaker beings, to be either ruled or guarded."

"Did you see me as someone to be ruled, or someone to be guarded? When I was still human, I mean."

"Honestly? Guarded, at first, but that was mainly because you were in danger and hurt. Once you healed, though, I saw how strong and independent you were, and I realized you would never settle for being ruled *or* being guarded."

I ponder this for a moment. "Is that because I'm an Alpha-type person?"

"A true Alpha now, in every sense. I suppose it's possible. It could just be your unique self."

"And a pack can only have one Alpha, unless they're a couple." I step out of Holden's arms. He feels so good when he's against me, but I can't give him that kind of commitment. I love Holden, yes, but I love each of his brothers just as much. I could never choose just one, not when they each fill my heart and body in a different way, and each matters just as much to me as the others.

Holden smells of sorrow again. I don't like the

smell of sorrow. Kind of like if mold smelled sad.

"That's the tradition. That's the way it's always been."

I turn and look up at him through my lashes. "Is it tradition because of how Alpha magic works, or is it tradition for tradition's sake?"

He starts to reach for me but stops himself. I don't think he knows how to handle me now that I'm a fellow Alpha wolf. Even if the confusion wasn't evident in his drawn brows and that slight frown, I can smell it.

"I can't answer that. I don't really know."

Hm. So, it could just be some lame "this is the way it's always been, and you'll do things this way and like it" kind of deals. Guess wolves aren't so different from humans after all.

What could be the worst that would happen if I stayed but didn't commit to Holden—if I didn't commit to any one wolf here? Holden and I might butt heads, sure, both being Alphas and all, but that's kind of like any relationship. Surely couldn't be worse than being controlled by Eric. At least I'd have my individuality, my sense of self, my dignity.

I'm getting ahead of myself, though. We've reached a point in the conversation where all the brothers need to be together, where we need to discuss this as a group. A family. As a pack.

"Let's go back to the others. I need to talk to all of you."

Holden drops his gaze, and his shoulders sag. He nods, and the sorrow-scent mingles with another murky, thick smell: grief.

Chapter 20

Back in the great room, the scent of grief fills the air — five times as strong as in the bathroom with Holden alone. It permeates so thick that I cough and cover my nose to try to filter some of it out.

"Okay, guys, you've gotta stop with this. I'm still not used to the super smell thing, and right now you *all* smell like someone died." Shame — which smells a little skunky — mixes with the grief, and I gag on the combination. "Ugh, just stop! None of you even know what I'm going to say, and you're all smelling like I'm going to haul my bike out of the garage and speed away any second, never to return. That's *not* going to happen, so please, calm the fuck down."

A chorus of mumbled "sorry"s follows. The air clears up a little bit, and I can breathe again.

"Right. So, here's how I understand things so far: I have apparently become a shifter — " I look to Holden to be sure I've got the right word; he nods " — by uh, let's just say by being around you guys so much. Which, I guess, is some super rare thing. And the Cherry on top of this particular sundae is that I'm also an Alpha, which traditionally throws a wrench into things pack-wise, unless I partner with the Alpha of the pack. How am I doing on the rundown?"

The Hunter brothers all nod and mutter affirmations.

I start pacing in the middle of the room. "Cool. So

here's where I'm going to put my offer on the table. I don't want to leave you guys. Ever. I like it here, and I love you all to death. All of you. You're all special to me, and that's where I think your tradition of strict Alpha pairings is complete and utter bullshit."

Shock smells funny. Kind of like the scent in the air after a fireworks show. A little singed, like I just blew a fuse in their brains and I'm smelling the burnt wires. I stop pacing and meet each gaze, one by one, until I'm sure I've got their full attention.

"Here's my proposal: I say we throw pack tradition out the fucking window. Screw this B.S. about Alphas and rules and all that shit. What do you guys say to me joining the pack as-is? No strings, no commitments, no rules. Just go on living here like I have been. I'll stay in the guest room, unless I choose to sleep in someone else's room for a night or two. No one will own anyone else. All open, all up front. Above board."

More burnt wires, plus some hesitation, some eagerness, and a heavy dose of doubt and concern. Geiger recovers from the shock of my proposition first, and he frowns. "Cherry, we can't have two Alphas in the pack unless they're paired. It doesn't work like that."

"Why the fuck not? Have I ever said or done anything to flat-out contradict something Holden did or didn't want you to do? Without good reason, anyway."

"Well, no ..."

"Right. So if the two Alphas are generally in agreement about things, why can't there be two?"

Wow. Dumbstruck has a scent. Who knew?

"Okay, then. It's the fucking twenty-first century

here, guys. I, for one, think we can all live here together in harmony. We can all be together, in our own way, and say 'fuck it' to the rules." I stand in the dead center of the room and hold my hand out, like I'm a quarterback waiting for the team to rally together at the pre-game huddle. "Who's with me?"

Holden joins the huddle first. He puts his hand over mine and gazes into my eyes. "I have no issues with you, and I have no issues with a two-Alpha pack. I agree to your terms."

Geiger gets up next, and I realize they're going in order of pack hierarchy.

"If you both will take me as your Beta, I will gladly join your pack."

Matt, Rick, and Billy follow suit, until we're all six standing in a circle, holding hands. Though I started this with my usual snark and bitchiness, the moment has a solemn feel to it, like we're sealing an unbreakable pact. I stare at our pile of hands, and something deep inside me takes over. I throw my head back and let loose with a lupine howl, and my packmates all howl with me. The air buzzes with what I now recognize as the pack magic, and now that I'm a wolf I can distinguish each pack member's individual wolf within the "hum," as Holden called it.

The beauty of it all, combined with the love I feel, see, and smell from each wolf, brings tears to my eyes. One of those salty buggers breaks free and slides down my cheek, and Geiger catches it with his hand.

"Funny, you don't smell sad," he says.

I sniffle and nuzzle his hand. "I'm not. I'm so fucking happy right now." My voice breaks with the force of emotion behind my words, and a laughing sob bubbles out of me as more tears spring forth. "Oh, God, I was trying so hard to be cool about this, and now the fucking waterworks have started."

The wolves surround me with their arms in a mass hug. I drink in their scents and revel in their warmth.

My pack.

Once the crying stops, I step back and take a moment to catch my breath. "Okay, so I guess there's only one thing left for me to do, right?"

Holden exchanges glances with his brothers, and they all frown. "What's that?"

I make a sweeping gesture at the group. "I need to get my own tattoo! You all look badass with yours. I feel left out with my pale, empty skin."

Everyone bursts out laughing. Matt claps me on the shoulder with a wicked grin on his face. "Do you know what you want?"

I pause to think about it. I'd need something meaningful. Maybe a couple of tattoos, really. One just wouldn't be enough. I'd need something to represent me, and something else to represent the pack bond. "I know one for sure. Maybe another later, but I need to think on it more."

"Well," Holden says, rubbing his stubbled chin, "our artist is usually open pretty late, and if ever there was a reason to go out and celebrate with a commemorative tattoo, this here's a pretty good one." He winks and grins, showing off his dimples. "And if you need one drawn up, he can do that for us, too. You can get the one today, then the other when he's got it all designed for you."

"Sweet! Let's go now and grab some food on the way. I'm starving."

We all file into the van, which has been hosed down and vacuumed inside. The only remnant of the blood from earlier is a faint coppery smell beneath the scent of bleach and cleanser. The excitement emanating from the others smells sort of like buttered popcorn, with a hint of something spicy.

The drive-thru teller at Billy Bob's Steak and Chicken Emporium gawks when he hands us our ten bags of food. Being a wolf, I've discovered, makes one hungrier than usual. I devour my two T-bones before we make it through three stop lights.

Holden watches me in the rearview mirror. "Yeah, the healing magic will do that. You expended a lot of energy, so your body's trying to recoup."

"Whatever," I mumble through a mouthful of fries. "Just keep your eyes the road."

The van's brakes squeal when it pulls to a stop in the tattoo parlor's lot. I yank open the sliding door and hop out first, then slam it shut before Matt, Rick, or Billy can follow me. Geiger, who's got the passenger door halfway open, gives me a puzzled stare.

"I'm doing this on my own. I've got some cash. I'll go in, get the tat, and call you guys when I'm done." I wink. "Go run some errands or something! Go shopping, whatever. I happen to know that at least three of you owe me new underwear. Go pick me out something cute. I'm willing to wager you scoped my size when you were raiding my apartment, Geiger."

To my surprise, Geiger blushes. "It was just in case you needed new clothes."

I stretch up and give him a kiss on the cheek. "You're adorable. Go. Kill some time. I'll call you guys later."

With that, Geiger shuts his door, and the van pulls away.

I'm in luck; the shop is empty of other customers, and the tattoo artist—a skinny, rockabilly-looking dude named Steve—says he doesn't have any appointments for the next two hours. More than enough time.

The artist snorts when he reads my I.D. after I tell him what I want today. "You sure you just want one? Ninety-nine percent of these are done in pairs."

"Just the one," I say. "With a little burning fuse instead of a stem."

"And you want it over that scar there?"

I pull my hair back and stretch my neck as I look in the mirror he holds up for me. "Hm. Yeah, right there. Like, maybe the fuse meets it right at the scar? Oh! Make the scar the fuse! I mean, it's a little longer than a stem would be, but … yeah! Can you do that?"

"Hell, I can do damn near anything you want." He grabs a pair of black synthetic gloves and puts them on, then takes a thin package out of a container on his desk. Inside the package is a marker, which he uses to draw directly on my skin. "There a story to this little number here?" he asks as he sketches.

"Mm-hm."

"Cool. Well, whatever the story is, I think it's cool that you survived it. That's badass. This shit goes right across your jugular." He nibbles at the ring in his lip as he works, and I do my best to hold still until he gives me a nod that I can talk again.

"I'm tougher than I look."

"No doubt, Cherry. Here's the mirror again. What do you think?"

I inspect the purple outline he's drawn and grin. "I

love it!"

"Sweetness. Let me get set up here, then."

An hour and a half later, I call Matt's phone to tell
the pack that I'm done. When they come to pick me up,
Matt opens the sliding door with a grin, but it soon
drops to a pout when he sees that my tattoo is covered
with a bandage. "What, we can't see it yet?"

I jerk a thumb back towards the shop. "Steve said
to keep it covered for an hour before I wash it and put
more ointment on." I hold up a sheet of paper the tattoo
artist gave me. "Aftercare instructions. Surely you all
know how this works?"

Holden laughs from his spot in the driver's seat.
"Cherry, you can heal that in, like, five minutes. Just do
the same thing we did last night. A tat heals a *lot*
quicker than a sprained ankle, some broken bones, and
a head injury. You don't even need to go to sleep for
something that small."

"Really? Cool." I climb in and sit in the back
between Rick and Billy. I close my eyes to concentrate,
and the Alpha buzz zeroes in on my fresh wound.

Holden was right; about five minutes later, I feel
the healing finish. The buzzing tingle fades, followed
by a brief flash of itching, and I peel off the bandage.
Geiger turns around in his seat to get a look, and even
Holden peeps in the rearview. He takes a water bottle
out of the cup holder and hands it back. "Matt, take this
and some of the napkins from dinner and wipe that
down. I want to get a better look, and the dried blood
and smeared ink are in the way."

"You *should* be watching the road." I chide him as
Matt cleans me up.

When Matt's done, he sits back and whistles.

"That's fucking awesome. I love how you had him work it into your scar there."

Billy takes one look and breaks out in song. "Ch-ch-ch-cherry bomb!"

"Damn skippy," I say, and I grin so wide it hurts my face. "Cut me, and I will light up and explode on your ass."

"That's so fucking hot, Cherry." I smell arousal with Holden's words, thick and musky.

"Would you watch the damn road? I've been through enough shit in the past few days; I don't need to survive all that just to die in an accident because you weren't paying attention to traffic."

Holden sighs and flips the turn signal for the road home.

As the van bumps down the winding forest road, I take out my phone for a selfie with my new tattoo. Not that I'll be on social media much anymore, what with being wanted for two murders, but I want a pic. I turn on the front-facing camera and pull my hair back with my free hand. It takes a minute to get the angle right, but I finally get a good shot of it.

My scar from Eric's first attempt on my life — which, after two major Alpha healings, is much thinner and smaller — now looks like a raised rope, with a small flame burning it at the top near my ear and a bright red cherry at the bottom, on the side of my throat.

"So what's next, Ms. Cherry Bomb?" Billy grins wide, and I grin back.

"Cuddle pile in Cherry's bed?" I say with a raised brow. "Everyone here is invited. I think we could all use a good, peaceful night's rest for once."

Matt chimes in. "You don't think that would be

weird? I mean, we're all brothers. What if you decide you want to get a little more than cuddly with one of us, if you get my drift?"

I reach up and ruffle Matt's hair. "No one's getting lucky tonight, bucko. Not even me. I just need to have you all snuggled up with me. I think it's an Alpha thing. I feel the need to gather you all in a space that's 'mine' and just keep you there for a while."

"Sounds about right," Holden says as he turns into the driveway and presses the garage door opener. "Totally an Alpha thing."

I send the boys off to get into some pajama bottoms at the very least, because I know I won't be able to keep my cuddle pile platonic if any of them are naked, and I change into some comfy flannel pajamas myself. I get into the middle of my bed and wait.

One by one, the wolves file in, in pack order. Holden crawls over me to lie between me and the wall, Geiger gets on my other side, and Matt, Rick, and Billy all find spots to nuzzle in and touch me. I've got hot men all over me, but that's not what's the best thing. The best thing is the scent of pure love and contentment. Soft, flowery, and a little sweet.

This. I could live this life for a thousand years and die happy.

Tomorrow I'll have to try my hand at shifting.
<The End>

About the Author

AJ Mullican is the author of self-published bestseller *Whispers of Death*, a psychosexual supernatural thriller, and *Abnormal*, the first in a series of sci-fi/dystopian novels, published by RhetAskew Publishing. The second in the series, *Escaping the Light*, is due out later this year–COVID-permitting, that is …

AJ is also a contributing author in the international bestsellers *Wicked Souls: A Limited Edition Reverse Harem Romance Collection, Hexes and Handcuffs: A Limited Edition Collection of Supernatural Prison Stories,* and *Askew Ever After: A Contemporary Romance Collection.*

After dipping into romance, AJ threw herself into a collection of paranormal romance novellas, *The Mage Asylum Trilogy: Palmore's Home for Wayward Mages Paranormal Romance Collection*. Her new paranormal romance series, *Bargains Struck*, a trilogy of standalone shared-universe reverse harem novels, starts with this book.

When not writing, AJ can be found fencing with live (though blunted) steel swords and participating in historical reenactment (pre-1600). Embroidery is her other passion (when she's not writing), and she is nearly entirely self-taught from Pinterest tutorials. She lives in southern Arizona with her husband and two cats, Rory and River. AJ also enjoys dabbling in cosplay and can often be found at signings or conventions dressed up to display her nerdery for all to see–when there's not a global pandemic to deal with, of course ...

Made in the USA
Monee, IL
03 November 2020